SMARTY

There's nothing really wrong with Stanley Martin Martinson; he just seems to be forgettable. He lacks that certain something that would make the girl who sits two rows ahead of him in History remember his name. He's the last one to get told about a great party over the weekend, if he gets told at all.

But Marty isn't dumb — they don't call him "Smarty" for nothing — and he devises a plan to earn his classmates' attention. With the skeptical but loyal help of his best friend, Lester, he decides to take action and become "someone."

Filled with honest affection for its characters and setting, *Smarty* is the story of how any worm can turn.

It helps if the worm has brains and a plan.

SMARTY

Arthur S. Rosenblatt

Little, Brown and Company

BOSTON TORONTO

FIRST EDITION

Library of Congress Cataloging in Publication Data

Rosenblatt, Arthur S.
  Smarty.

  Summary: Marty, a "smart" but forgettable kid in
the seventh grade, makes his bid for attention when
he decides to run for president against the most
popular boy in his class.
  [1. School stories]   I. Title.
PZ7.R71916Sm   [Fic]   81-12412
ISBN 0-316-75720-9   AACR2

BC
*Published simultaneously in Canada
by Little, Brown & Company (Canada) Limited*

PRINTED IN THE UNITED STATES OF AMERICA

for
D & E
&
EFB

SMARTY

Chapter 1

Ching!
    Ching! Ching!
One nickel after another dropped into the fare box.
Ching!
Water streaming down his yellow slicker, the last passenger plodded down the aisle to the empty seat in the rear as the bus pulled away from the curb.

Stanley Martin Martinson, Jr., plopped down and gazed at the blurred images that appeared outside the splattered, steamy window. He was glad he would only have two short blocks to walk when he got off. He usually walked the whole way home from school, but it was well worth five cents to ride on a stormy day like this. He'd be there soon, and he'd be there dry. He'd come in the back way and his mother would tell him to hang his wet things in the bathroom. Then he'd sit down in the kitchen with a hot cup of cocoa in front of him. And he'd have a few Toll House cookies from the elf-face jar on top of the

3

refrigerator. And then he'd get out his Captain Midnight decoding ring and start to figure out . . .

" 'Scuse me," said the plump blonde girl with the ponytail as she made her way through the crowd. She reached the back of the bus and wedged into the seat next to him.

Searching for an opening in the folds of her soggy raincoat, she reached in and found a crumpled, dainty pink handkerchief with lace edges. Carefully mopping her damp face, she turned to gaze at the still raging rainstorm and finally she noticed the familiar boy sitting next to her.

"Oh, I didn't even recognize you for a minute," she said as she adjusted the schoolbag on her lap. "You're 'Martinson, Jr.'; I'm 'Tracey, Marilyn Tracey,' we're in Social Studies together. Fourth period."

"Right, right. And it's 'Marty,' a little shorter and lot easier," he replied.

"And here comes Muriel Markey, poor Muriel," she announced at the sight of a dripping form struggling down the aisle bearing an enormous armload of books and notebooks. "Looks like we have half the class back here," she laughed.

"Not quite," said Martin, quickly adding, "but as far as things go, it's two to one; the girls lead."

Did that sound dumb? he wondered. Well, what else could you say? Maybe she thought it was clever. It was supposed to be. Besides, isn't that the kind of thing everyone said all the time? Sure sounded like

4

it to him. Too bad Lester wasn't there to fill in the dull spots. His friend Lester was real good at that. But today was the day he stayed after classes for his clarinet lesson. Lester's mother claimed he was musical. Everyone said she was about the only person who thought so.

Marilyn whispered, "I don't know why she lugs all those books around. She gets such bad marks, I don't even think she opens them. And her mother makes her stay in her room all the time. She can't even go out after supper, not even when it's still light out, before Daylight Saving Time ends. I never have anything to say to her. Oh, hi, Muriel!" she called across the aisle.

"Hi, Marilyn, oh . . . hi . . . umm . . . Tom . . . uh . . ." and her voice trailed off.

"Hi, yourself, *Muriel*," he replied, disappointed that she didn't remember his name. After all, he came right behind her alphabetically and he had spent the first weeks of junior high school staring at the back of her head. Weren't they both in Beginners' French as well as Social Studies? He was good in both subjects, too. He usually answered a lot of questions, so she had plenty of opportunities to hear the teachers call his name out loud. Plenty. Maybe she had a weak memory for names. She certainly had a weak memory for history.

"Listen, Muriel, did you see those funny book-covers they're selling at the stationery store just

5

around the corner from the drugstore?" Marilyn asked.

"You mean the plastic ones with the colored pictures?" replied Muriel. "I hear they have real paintings of movie stars. I wonder if they have Errol Flynn. He's kind of *old*, but I love Errol Flynn," she sighed.

Sitting there in his shiny yellow slicker, his curly hair still damp under the edges of his cap, Martin felt trapped as the bus rattled and the girls prattled on. Even if he tried to get into their conversation, he wouldn't know what to say. What did he know about sales on book-covers or shampoo or bobby pins or whatever else they were gabbing about?

". . . so I can't even go to cheering practice and I don't know whether I'll be able to make the big rally on Friday, either," Muriel complained as she opened a package of Juicy Fruit gum, put two pieces in her mouth, and handed a third to Marilyn.

What rally? thought Martin.

"I didn't know they announced it," said Marilyn, carefully unwrapping the stick of gum. "They usually don't put out a notice till the day before."

"They haven't," replied Muriel, chomping away and perfuming the air with the sweet smell of tropical fruits, "but everybody knows. I mean, *we* all know. You knew, didn't you, Marilyn?"

Crack, snapped the gum across the aisle.

"Of course," purred Marilyn. "I'm glad it's Friday

6

so I won't have to stay in and study. That's probably where you'll be," she added smugly. She suddenly turned to Martin. "And you, too, Martinson. He's so smart, Muriel, he doesn't really have to study, but I'll bet he grinds away just to keep ahead of everyone else, huh?"

Before Martin could speak up, Muriel lashed back, "Oh yeah? Well, that shows how much you know. I may be going to the rally, and my mother might even give me permission to stay out late for the roller-skating party."

Roller-skating party? What roller-skating party? Martin wondered.

Who was *we?* How did *we* find out about these things? Where did they get started? And why didn't he ever hear about them at the beginning? Did he study too much? Did he keep to himself too much? Everyone on the bus seemed to have lots of friends, except him. Why was he feeling sort of empty, sort of left out? Sort of . . . alone.

He glanced to his left: there were kids laughing, joking with one another, "I made-ja look, I made-ja look, I made-ja steal a dirty-book."

He turned to the right: more kids gabbing away, poking one another playfully. "C'mon, Barry, cut it out. You wanna use my English Raleigh, huh?"

He stared through the dark glass at the gray world outside. Damp and uncomfortable on the hot, crowded bus, Martin felt his stomach slowly begin

7

to knot. Going to school was supposed to be more than just studying. It was supposed to be having fun and friends and doing things. But for all anyone cared, he might as well be back in the classroom with his nose stuck in a book. He felt invisible, like a ghost.

Well, that does it. I've been a ghost too long, darn it. I've made up my mind. This time I'm going to do something about it. Right away. Tomorrow.

And then it came to him. A light bulb seemed to turn on over his head, just like in the comics. He didn't have to be left out, to be the one who never knew what was happening. All he had to do was . . . yes, just that.

Martin's home was an apartment in a three-story building in the Glendale section of Greater Boston. Glendale had once been a fashionable place to live for people who worked downtown. It was an easy ride by bus or trolley to the subway and from there right into the heart of the city. But times changed. Another town became fashionable and Glendale became poorer and more crowded. Real estate speculators bought up large lots and built big apartment buildings right next to small private houses. The result was a helter-skelter arrangement of rows of uneven tall, square brick boxes towering over squat clapboard homes. Martin often thought his own block looked a lot like a jack-o'-lantern's smiling teeth.

A few of the remaining private houses were converted into smaller apartment units, called flats. The Martinsons lived in one of these flats — two and three-fourths bedrooms, living room, kitchen, pantry, and bathroom carved out of the middle of the upstairs parlor and dining room of a single-family house. "Could have put up the Russian army with all the room they had up here," Mrs. Martinson often said.

In the early years of their marriage, Mr. and Mrs. Martinson lived downtown, close to his work in the Atlantic Avenue wholesale fish market. But after he came back from World War II, Mr. Martinson was anxious to be on his own and eventually he found a good location for a fish market in Glendale. There he opened his shop and, shortly afterward, the whole Martinson family moved to Glendale and settled in.

One chilly October morning, Mr. Martinson gathered up his lunch box and glanced at the kitchen clock as he got ready to leave for work. Four A.M. It seemed earlier and earlier, all the time. But the early bird got the best pick of the catch, right? He yawned, stretched, and headed for the door when: BANG! he accidentally knocked over the wastebasket.

"Rats," he muttered. Just his luck he'd wake his daughter, Helena. He listened. No, there seemed to be no sound coming from her room, where he knew she lay dreaming cotton candy fantasies of movie stars, or of a date with Rick Petersen, the local football star. He smiled. Helena's "crushes" were legion,

9

but this one had lasted longer than most. He wondered if the Petersen boy had any idea of the role he played in Helena's imagination.

Still grinning, he glanced at the door next to Helena's. Less complicated dreams in there, he thought. There was no fear of waking Martin. His son was one of the great deep sleepers.

Burrowed under his blankets, Martin usually gave the impression that he wouldn't budge until the winter was over and the Red Sox were on their way back from Florida. But, at the first sound of his Little Ben alarm clock, he would jump out of bed with surprising energy, ready to take on the new day.

Not that morning.

"Martin," his mother called from the kitchen. "Martin, get up, you'll be late for school."

Martin didn't slide off the bed and rush into the bathroom as usual. This morning he clenched his eyes tight, faced the wall, and curled deeper into the pillow. He was clearly not ready to rise and shine and face the day.

The smell of warm milk drifted into the room and the sound of footsteps approached.

"What on earth are you doing there? Didn't you hear me call you? Twice, already? Look, I don't have time to bother with this. Now get up and get going; your cereal's almost on the table." She threw open his door expecting to see the usual orderly arrangement of books, sporting equipment, and clothing. If Martin had faults, sloppiness wasn't one of them. She had effectively planted and her children had readily absorbed certain virtues. "Cleanliness Is Next to Godliness" and "Neatness Counts" didn't need picture frames; they were carved into the children's brains.

But today she discovered a royal mess. Crumpled wads of arithmetic paper shared floor space with Martin's discarded socks and underwear. Yesterday's shirt and trousers, inside out, were stretched across his armchair. Even the radio, his beloved radio, was almost buried under the mountain of rubbish that covered every available surface. His room had never looked like this before, even at the height of the sixth grade Open House project with the gerbils. And that, she thought, was bad enough.

She drew a breath and was about to launch into an award-winning scolding when she thought, Maybe there was something wrong with him. Was he sick? She had bent over to feel his forehead when the front doorbell began to ring.

"Martin, are you all right? Get up, please. I have to get the door.

"One minute," she called down the hallway. "Who's there?"

"It's Lester, Lester Lerner. Is Martin ready?" came the same reply that she heard every school morning.

And there he was. Eighty-six pounds of anxious preparation on a four-foot-three-inch frame. Over his shoulder Lester carried an enormous schoolbag filled with books, his lunch in a brown paper bag, and an assortment of useful tools to get him through the day. Within the waterproof lining of the green bag was an extra pair of eyeglasses in a snap-shut case, a clean handkerchief, several tattered notebooks of various sizes, a ball-point pen with its refillable cartridge, a jackknife with two blades (the smaller one broken), an unusually large pink eraser, several rubber bands in assorted sizes, a box of white Canada Mints, a badly worn rabbit's foot key chain with no keys, a miniature set of dominoes, and a dime-store compass. Lester was, if nothing else, prepared.

"Lester, what a surprise."

"Aw, Mrs. Martinson, you're kidding me." He grinned.

"Well, maybe I am. You come right in and sit down. Martin's a little slow this morning. So, you just have a seat and pour yourself a glass of milk if you want. I'll be right back."

She turned toward the bedrooms and Helena swept past her, fresh from the bathroom and smelling of expensive toilet water.

"I said you could use just a little of that, Missy. Go ahead and waste it and there'll be none till your next birthday. Now, no back talk. Get going and have your breakfast and talk to Lester, will you please?"

"Lester? What am I going to say to Lester?"

"Well, you could say, 'It's nice to see you this morning, Lester.' That'll give him such a shock you won't have to say another thing."

Helena groaned and Mrs. Martinson advanced toward Martin's room. The door was shut, but she could hear the noisy sound of drawers shutting and the closet door slamming, as well as the rustle of papers; obviously he was getting his clothes together and picking up that mess in a hurry.

Good, she thought, he isn't sick. But what on earth could lead to such a mess? No time for discussion now, especially in front of Lester. Well, I'll just wait till he gets home from school and then I'll give him something special, maybe a nice fresh slice of pie. Maybe I'll have time to make a batch of butterscotch pecan cookies.

To Mrs. Martinson, food wasn't just a necessity; it was medicine that could cure most of life's problems. A lemon meringue pie had dried many a tear and a pork roast stuffed with apricots had once healed the worst quarrel ever between Martin and Helena. Even she and Mr. Martinson worked out difficulties over a crisp potato pancake now and again.

I wonder if it's too early in the season to do something with cranberries, she thought.

Martin burst from the bedroom, half unbuttoned, and dashed into the bathroom.

"Don't forget to comb your hair. I'll just heat up that oatmeal a little. You're not leaving this house without your breakfast, young man. It takes a full stomach to get anywhere in this world, believe you me," she said.

She walked back into the kitchen. Lester, his upper lip adorned with a milk moustache, was gazing adoringly at Helena. Oblivious, Helena silently shoveled down her oatmeal with lightning speed.

"Kids," sighed Mrs. Martinson.

"Gee, Martin, how come you were so late this morning? You want to take the bus?"

"No, if we go through the back field we can get there OK. Let's run, I'll talk to you when we get down the hill. Last one there is a dirty Nazi."

"Hey, aren't they our friends now?" shouted Lester after him, as he set off in the same direction.

The back field was a ragged lot, the remains of a temporary housing development built quickly for returning World War II veterans and their families. It was supposed to be used for only one or two years, but many families had lived there much longer before moving on. When children born in that "G.I. project" started showing up in kindergarten, the city decided to tear down the barrackslike structures. The occupants were relocated and plans for future use of the back field were supposed to be drawn up.

But no one could agree on what should be built there, and the area gradually deteriorated. Fences were put up to keep the neighborhood children out, but they never worked. Kids always managed to find a way in. To them, it was just an open space to play. Only adults saw dangers in the place.

The lot, in fact, did hold plenty of small hazards. On their way through the back field, Martin and Lester circled blocks of old foundations, which jutted out from weeds and ragged bushes. They passed piles of discarded hot water heaters, old stoves, sinks, and toilets that formed rusting pyramids. In some areas they had to work their way carefully by overgrown brambles that mingled with tall grasses, waiting to trip them up. Scattered clumps of rubble surrounded barely visible hollows and pits. There was junk spread everywhere over the uneven ground. Many a game of "Rotten Eggs" or "Scatter" or "Ringalevio" was stopped abruptly by a sprained ankle or a bloody gash.

Still, when the sun shone, a sort of magical kingdom often emerged as tiny shafts of sunlight filtered through the clutter and touched the rotting hulks with gilt. Butterflies arose from the damp green grass and the stray bumblebee sometimes came in search of pollen among the touch-me-nots and fragrant ragweed.

And if you stuck to the cleared paths wherever

possible, it was still the fastest way to get to school. By cutting through the back field and darting down a small incline which interrupted the flat criss-cross of streets and avenues, the boys saved a good ten minutes.

Chapter 2

The William Howard Taft Junior High School was situated at the base of the hill, next to a man-made incline that supported a row of bleachers on the side of the playground–ball field. The field's edge was an open space large enough to accommodate a scrubby football field that ended abruptly in a large irrigation ditch.

Leaning up against the bleachers, the two boys caught their breath. They stood and watched the milling crowd of students start to drift into the many entrances to the school. Like ants going to work in the anthill, Martin thought.

"Hey, Bernie, how come you're not wearing your Yankees jacket anymore?" Martin shouted to the back of a tall redheaded boy. Involved in another conversation, Bernie didn't answer. " 'Cause they're losers, that's why," Martin mumbled to himself.

The first, warning bell began to ring. There was a full ten minutes before they had to be in their seats.

"So what's up, Martin?" panted Lester.

"OK, Lester, but before I say anything, remember when you first moved in last year? Remember how you came over to the stickball game and after we let you into the game you couldn't do anything right? I know, I know, you said you were nervous. But remember how I went in for Howie Harris and I pitched the last couple of innings and I gave you that meatball, I mean a real ice cream pitch and you got a hit right down the middle. And then everyone thought you weren't so bad, after all. And since then you get to hang out with the kids on our street and everything? Remember all that?"

"Sure," answered Lester, looking off across the field.

"Well, Les," Martin continued, "since then you've become my best friend, honest, and I really trust you. I've told you just about everything I've never told anyone else. Even about the time I saw Helena putting handkerchiefs in her brassiere."

"And I never told anyone anything you ever told me, did I? Did I?"

"No. Even so, for now you have to *swear* to me that what I'm going to tell you is our own private secret. It goes no further until I say it's OK to tell, all right? Swear and scrub?"

Lester blinked at his friend. Then he dutifully rubbed his knuckles in the dusty ground at his feet.

"Swear and scrub," he agreed.

"All right," Martin began, "here's what . . . I mean

not vote for you, but why *should* they? You know, huh? Why? What do you want to be president for, anyhow?"

"Come on, Les, you know that, well . . . it's hard to explain . . . but, it's just that, you see . . ." Martin hesitated. Then, brushing the hair off his forehead with the back of his hand, he blurted out, "Look, everyone knows the president of the class, just like everyone knows the President of the country. They respect him. And it doesn't matter anymore what things were like in the past, once you're in office, it's only what happens then that counts. It's like getting a new start on things."

"Geez, I never thought of that. You need a new start?"

"Yeah, I do. Don't you see, ever since I've been in school, for as long as I can remember, everyone expected that I would always be on the Honor Roll and get A's and everything, but no one ever paid much attention to anything else about me. They never tell me about parties or anything. But if I were president, they'd have to. I'd be more than just some kind of walking brain. Besides, Lester, to answer your question, I really think I could do a good job. I'm not exactly dumb, you know."

"Very funny, Martin. It sounds simple, but . . . I don't know. President? Hey, look, there's hardly anybody left out here. C'mon, we've gotta get into our homeroom now. We'll talk it over later. How much time do you have to put your name in? What did it say in the *Bulletin?*"

"One week from today."

At the sound of the bell, the Glendale morning began.

In the classroom the usual things were said. The usual thoughts were thought.

The teachers said:	*The students thought:*
Suppose a man is traveling on a train between Boston and New York at 100 miles per hour ...	I'd like to be on a train going to see the Giants play. . . .
Angela, can you tell us anything about the Louisiana Purchase?	Angie is so dumb. Probably thinks it's a kind of shopping trip.
If you will learn to use active verbs properly, your speech will improve.	There's a few choice active verbs I could tell her. . . .

In the Martinson household, the daily routine was underway. Martin had picked up most of the trash, but there were a few odds and ends left. Mrs. Martinson gathered them up along with his pajamas and started to make his bed. She wondered what could be on his mind. Her son was usually easy to read and she could generally see what he called Big

Doings creeping up before they actually started. Not this time, though.

Gingerly dusting around the stack of what had to be the world's largest collection of baseball cards, she wondered how she would get to the bottom of this one. Scolding wouldn't help, she knew. That boy would just look straight through her as though there wasn't a thing wrong in the world. . . . Lamb chops were one way to soften up her husband, and a double-rich chocolate *anything* would always do the trick with Helena. But Martin didn't have that many real favorites. Except . . . except. Yes, and this was the right time of year. A nice, fresh applesauce cake. Maybe with spice frosting. She went to the kitchen. Perhaps a little piece when he came home from school. While the radio ad told her that Tide In meant Dirt Out, she checked her cupboard for nutmeg and cinnamon.

Down on Shirley Street, Mr. Martinson took a sip of his midmorning coffee before returning to the halibut he was cutting up into fillets. He carefully guided his knife around the bones and then slowly stripped off the skin. The bell above the door jingled and he turned to see Tom Sweeney in his blue uniform and leather shoulder sack placing a small pile of envelopes on the showcase.

"Thanks, Tom," he called over his shoulder. "Did you bring me anything besides bills?"

"C'mon, Stan, you know I never look. But there is one swell card with one *swell* blonde on it."

"Wow, I wonder who likes me that much," Mr. Martinson said as he glanced at it. "Oh, it's from my Thursday lobster, Dolly Sutter. You know her? She lives up in the Heights, but she's been coming here for years. Her husband works late on Thursdays. So, when she eats alone, she treats herself to a lobster. They took a trip last week and she said she'd send me something special to make up for the lobster she hadn't bought. It must be some place, Denmark, if they all look like this there!"

He reached down and took a thumbtack from a cigar box of odds and ends. Up went the postcard and the blonde smiled mutely in the middle of a collection of business cards from plumbers, painters, stockbrokers, and insurance agents — and a free coupon for half-price bowling at Marco's Bowladrome, any time from 11:00 P.M. to 1:00 A.M. He glanced at the card again, grinned, and went back to the halibut.

In Room 307, in her class in Ancient History, Helena was trying hard to concentrate. She focused on the generals marching forth to the Trojan War, but her mind kept drifting. Standing on the lofty towers, she saw herself gazing down at thousands of men dueling with one another to protect her honor. Her eyes rested on her champion, Paris. Through the dust cloud he looked just like Rick Petersen. He was advancing toward her, all the way from ancient Greece. She even heard him call her name. . . .

"Helena," came the cry, "Helenaaaaaa . . ."

"Helena, please pay attention. Tell the class the chief causes of the rift which evolved into . . . ," Miss Collins continued as the vast difference in time was bridged and Helena fumbled to find an answer.

The voice squawking over the intercom belonged to the principal's secretary, Miss Bellini. In high-pitched, nasal tones came the request, "Will you please send S. M. Martinson, Jr., to the office as soon as possible. Thank you."

The murmurs and snickers began almost immediately.

"Oh, boy, here's where Martinson gets it."

"I'll send you a cake with a file in it, pal."

"You wanna name of a good lawyer?"

The whole World Geography class sent him off with a general sigh of sympathy. Did a request to go to the office ever mean anything good? he wondered. What do they want me for? What have I done? No major crimes came to mind. Even his few small infractions of school rules didn't seem important enough for a call in the middle of a class. Then, the number of candy wrappers he had tossed carelessly on the school grounds started to grow larger in his mind. Was that it?

He became more and more nervous as, under the glare of bright fluorescent lights, he walked up to the high counter separating the oily mimeograph machine, the gray file cabinets, and the teachers' dark brown mailboxes. He noticed the arm raised on the paper cutter above the counter. It looked sharp and lethal, capable of chopping off a head. Or a tongue, even. What other instruments of torture were hidden below? Was that a closet over there, or did that door lead to a room with a single light bulb and a stool where they tied you down and dripped water on your shaven head till you admitted that it was you who drew "Kilroy Was Here" pictures on the divider walls of the boys' toilets?

Miss Bellini rose from her desk and stood with her back to the big green window shades that were drawn against the morning sun. Through the cracks on the sides, illuminated tiny specks danced about wildly in shafts of light. Miss Bellini spread her thin lips, smiled coldly, and announced that he was to go right in.

Behind the heavy door, the principal's oak-paneled office was varnished and polished so bright it shimmered.

"Have a seat, Stanley . . . er . . . Martin; it says you are called 'Martin' in your file here," said Mr. Lindstrom, the principal. Buttoned snugly into his vested suit, his starched white shirt collar cutting slightly into his fleshy neck, he seemed plump and jolly. But the watery blue eyes behind his thick glasses were cold as he glanced up from the manila folder in front of him. There was no smile on his face, just a hard line dividing his tightly drawn lips.

This doesn't look good, Martin thought.

"Well," Mr. Lindstrom went on, "we have been looking over your record from elementary school and some of the work you've done since you started here at Taft. You're doing exceptionally well in several of your subjects and seem to be having no difficulty adjusting to the larger environment of junior high school. In fact, you seem to be getting along fine."

He paused and cleared his throat. Martin saw the rolls above his collar jiggle and smothered the impulse to laugh. Maybe this wasn't going to be bad, after all.

Mr. Lindstrom even seemed to warm up a little. "In one of your subjects you are obviously capable of doing advanced work beyond the seventh-grade level. We feel that your present mathematics class appears to offer no challenge to you at all. So, we have decided to move you ahead in this one area. Starting next week you will report to your new assignment. Of course, we will need your parents' approval, but I have no doubt that they will agree with us that this is in your best interests."

Slam. Bam. Wham. *We* think this and *we're* doing that. No instruments needed here. All *we* need is in those files.

"But, Mr. Lindstrom . . . uh . . . sir . . . uh, don't you think it's too soon to tell? I mean, I've only been doing seventh-grade math for a few weeks. I mean, I don't know whether I ought to change so soon,"

27

Martin offered as a protest. He knew it was weak, but he was frantically searching for good reasons to stay where he was.

Everyone thought he was too smart for his own good as it was. What would they think if he skipped ahead right at the start of the school year . . . before . . . before Halloween! It could really mess up his new plans. But that kind of explanation would never go over with the principal, he knew.

"Now, Martin, your humility is understandable, but I think we know best in these matters. We've dealt with similar cases before and we've been proved right time and again."

We. We. We. Every *"we"* felt like an arrow whizzing into his chest. Martin grasped for more reasons to stall the move, but it was useless.

With a few concluding remarks about the new class that Martin would attend, Mr. Lindstrom folded his hands and nodded. Martin understood the gesture and left the office.

Chapter 3

No lines were drawn. No partitions existed. No color coding. No assigned seats. Yet as regularly as the rising of the sun and the flowing of the tides, each year new classes discovered their own particular section of the cafeteria and within that section their own group: athletes at one end, the loud and popular types in one girls' corner, the shy ones in the other; on that side, near the serving line, the poor kids who wolfed down the low-cost cafeteria meals; and finally, the dawdlers, the latecomers who ended up sitting next to the trash barrels, in front of the "Return Trays Here" sign.

And from each section voices bubbled up and filled the air. Fragments of conversation rose, pierced through the clutter, and then disappeared as newer, brighter, or more strident tones took over.

"My uncle didn't even know. . . . We were watching them cream the Rams when I had to go. . . . Her new compact was stolen. . . . Whaddya read after the funnies? . . . Better let them know in case I don't get to rehearsal. . . . Don't forget. . . . Hey, Stevie, where did you get that shirt? Salvation Army? . . . She gave us three whole chapters to read for Thursday! . . . Oh, rats, peanut butter and creamed cheese again. I think my mother hates me. . . ."

Lester was already seated at the end of a long trestle table in the middle of the seventh-grade section when Martin arrived with his brown lunch bag and a container of milk. It was Monday. That meant the cafeteria served a choice of creamed chicken or a dried-out hamburger on half a bun. The menu usually listed these items as "Henhouse Fricassee" and "Swiss Beef Patty on Rusk." Sometimes they were called "Ragout of Chicken Jardiniere" or "Chopped Steak Polonaise." No matter what the names were, they always looked — and tasted — the same. Lousy. Both boys preferred to take their chances on leftovers from their family dinners.

"Whatcha got, Martinson?" asked Howie Harris from one end of the table as he bit into his own ham and Swiss sandwich. "Wanna trade a half?"

"No, thanks, I'll stick with this," replied Martin. He carefully unwrapped a bulky waxed-paper package and took out a crisp roll spread with mustard and cradling thin slices of corned beef. Across the table, Lester had already begun to munch away, and his teeth were oozing what looked like pale blood.

Martin gasped. "What the heck is wrong with you? And what's that pink junk in your hand?"

"Phidd's gwy hwanglidgch," mumbled Lester, swallowing, then explaining, "I mean, it's my lunch, my turkey sandwich."

"What kind of color is that for turkey? What did they do to it, beat it to death?"

"Aw, c'mon," Lester went on. "That's just 'cause there's cranberry sauce on it. My mother wouldn't put on mayonnaise like I wanted. She's afraid it'd spoil in my locker and then poison me. See, there's nothing wrong with it," as he swallowed the last bite.

"Well, it looked just like puke, that's what," muttered Martin gruffly.

"That's rotten and you know it. What's eating you?" complained Lester. Then softly, "Is it 'cause of the election? Are you giving up already? We haven't even really talked it over. But I've been doing some thinking, in case you're still going to run."

"It's not that, Lester. And I'm sorry for what I said, but you sure did look funny with that pink goo in your mouth. Now, wait, I'm not going to start on that again, don't worry. But I've got something else to tell you now. Something I don't think is going to help with the election. I just got called down to the principal's office this morning."

"What?"

"Not because I did anything wrong. Oh, no, *worse*

31

than that." He went right into the story of his meeting with Mr. Lindstrom, gave Lester all the details he could remember, and finished, "So they're kicking me out of seventh-grade math and you'll never guess where I'm going."

"Where else, eighth grade?"

"Wrong. Ninth."

"Ninth-grade math, wow! You must be a genius or something."

"Don't get carried away, Lester. I'm really good at math and I have a terrific memory, that's all. They wanted to move me ahead a couple of times before, whole grades, but my folks don't believe in that. They think it's more important to grow up and go to school with kids your own age. So I guess this is how the school gets its own way. I'm still in the seventh grade, but I'm in ninth-grade math," he explained.

"Are you scared?" Lester asked.

"Not of the work. I can probably handle that. But I don't know how everyone else in our class will take it. And who do I know in—" He was interrupted by the sound of a luncheon tray crashing to the floor in the middle of the eighth-grade section. Spoons began to bang on tabletops, and catcalls, whistles, and applause spread throughout the cafeteria.

"Whew, glad that wasn't over here. The monitors will kill that kid," Martin observed as he continued. "Anyhow, I don't know whether the rest of the class, *our* class, will think I'm some kind of wise guy jumping ahead like that. It could hurt my chances in the election. It sure won't make it easier."

"But you're still going on with it, aren't you?" Lester asked.

Martin nodded. "I have to."

Lester was glad. When the Lerners had moved into the neighborhood a year ago, he and Martin had fallen into the habit of walking to school together and gradually got to be friends. Now, he could show that he was a *true* friend. He could help Martin with the election and, more than likely, he figured, he would share in some of the rewards. *If* Martin were elected.

So, with a firm, authoritative voice, he said, "OK, then we'd better have a strategy meeting. Why don't you come on over to my house after school and we'll figure out what we have to do. Meanwhile, keep your ears open and I'll do the same. We might find out how Normie plans to get votes. That is, before he knows who's running against him."

"Good idea," Martin replied. "You think he'll be worried about me?"

"Normie Sands? Are you for real? Listen, Martin, you're so good in math, you ought to be able to figure out the odds."

"Hey, Lester," said Martin.

"Huh?"

"Don't take any wooden nickels."

Chapter 4

There were two distinct areas in Mrs. Martinson's kitchen — the work area consisting of white enameled refrigerator and stove, the sink, the counter next to it, and the dining area with its sturdy wooden chairs and polished table top. No concrete barrier could create a stronger separation than the one she saw in the two parts of this single room.

At one time, Mr. Martinson had suggested that they buy a washing machine and dryer and put them in the "dining area." They could get by with a smaller table and chairs, he said.

"I'd sooner have lunch with Josef Stalin!" she replied, and continued to take the laundry to the automatic Self-Service four blocks away, pushing the bundles in the old wicker stroller that had once carried Helena and Martin around town.

It was Helena's job to set the table every evening in the dining area and to have everything ready on it by the time they were ready for supper.

"Those glasses aren't going to be much use without any water in them," Mrs. Martinson commented that evening as she approached the table with a large platter.

Helena flushed and got up to fill the pitcher as her mother sat down. She returned just as Mrs. Martinson began to distribute thick slices of salmon loaf to each plate. She didn't skimp on the servings she dished out. Her children had been raised to eat everything on their plates, including the fresh fish that was always available from her husband's store. If anyone, herself included, didn't clear his or her plate, three other voices were sure to chime in, "Remember the starving Armenians!"

"Looks bad for the Armenians tonight, Mom," said Helena, eyeing the steaming dish before her.

"They can't all be starving," said Mr. Martinson, "Matter of fact, I read about a fat one the other day. Seems they drove him out of town because he was creating the wrong impression."

"Really?"

"Helena, I think your father just got you. Sometimes I think you'll believe anything that man says." Mrs. Martinson smiled. Then she added, "A fat Armenian driven out of town. Imagine. As if those poor people hadn't suffered enough."

"Mmmmm, that's delicious," sighed Mr. Martinson as he tasted his first bite of the salmon loaf. "Could you pass me a piece of lemon, please, Martin? Martin? Are you with us?"

35

"Sure, Dad, I'm sorry, I was thinking of something else. Here's the salad."

"Thank you, but I only wanted the lemon, son." Mr. Martinson smiled.

Mrs. Martinson handed a dish of sliced lemons to her husband. Martin had dashed in and out so fast after school, just dropping off his books and announcing that he was going over to Lester's house for milk and cookies, that she hadn't had a chance to talk with him about the morning. The applesauce cake was still under wraps in the back of the cupboard waiting to entice him into revealing what was on his mind, but this might be a better opportunity.

"A penny for your thoughts, Martin," she offered.

"That's probably all they're worth," chimed in Helena.

"And that's enough out of you. Don't you two get started," her mother said quickly. "Martin, you just go ahead and pay no attention. Helena, I sat with you and helped you memorize all those old Greek and Roman names this afternoon. Now it's Martin's turn. Is there something going on at school, dear? Something you want to talk about?"

"Well," Martin said, "the principal talked to me today. He said they were going to put me into ninth-grade math, starting next Monday. And he said that if you want to talk to him about it, you could stop by any morning this week."

"Oh, no, Martin's going to be in my math class," groaned Helena. "I'm going to die!"

"Whoa! Wait a minute," Martin jumped in. "He said that I *wouldn't* be in the same one as you. There are three different groups, you know, and I'll be in one of the other two. And," he added, "Mr. Lindstrom said you were very good in math, too. It must run in the family."

Mr. Martinson laughed. "Well, your mother has always been a wizard at balancing our budget so I guess you must both take after her. Congratulations, I'm proud of you, son, but I don't know what will happen after this year. Where do you go next?"

"Oh, he said something about a tutorial program, a kind of special class. There's this citywide thing going on and he thinks I might be a part of it."

"Well, it can't hurt your chances of getting into a good college eventually and maybe winning a scholarship," reflected Mrs. Martinson. "So I think we should tell him we're all for it, don't you, Stan?"

"Sure, as long as it's OK with Martin. How do you feel about it? You don't look all that happy. Think you can handle it?"

"Oh, it's all right with me, I guess. I mean, I don't mind the work. It's just that I don't know how the kids in my class are going to take it."

"What do you mean?" asked Mrs. Martinson.

Martin paused. Helena was about to offer an opinion, but her mouth was filled with creamed onions. Before she could swallow, he said quickly, "I'm going to run for class president. You see, Lester and I talked it over and we figure I could get enough

37

votes if I do a little work, sort of campaign, because no one has anything against me except that I'm good in schoolwork and there are enough of my friends from elementary school in Taft now, and I don't have any real enemies. And I want to be elected. I want everyone in the class to get to know who I am. I feel like nobody knows me or includes me in anything now. I'd like to get in on all the good things going on and go to parties and everything and not be left out on the sidelines. *And* if I win the election, it will be a good start, I mean, it's hard to explain. But when everyone finds out about me jumping ahead in math, they're liable to think I'm a weirdo or some kind of brainy nut and that could hurt my chances." He paused and caught his breath.

His mother looked at her son. He was upset, but determined.

"This means a lot to you, dear, doesn't it?" she asked gently.

"I never wanted anything in school so much," he replied.

"Martin" — his father smiled at him — "I don't think the problem is as big as you imagine. And I suspect that you're going to find a way to handle it. I won't say, 'Don't worry,' but I will tell you not to lose any sleep over it. If there's anything we can do, not just your mother and me, but Helena, too, you just let us know."

"Look at Harry Truman," Helena offered, her

mouth onion-free. "Maybe you should 'give 'em hell!' "

"I think we can discuss political strategy later, Helena. And in nicer terms," said Mrs. Martinson. "Now, while I get dessert out of the cupboard, which future President of the United States wants to help by clearing the table?"

Martin laughed and looked pleased for the first time that day. Helena sat back and silently wondered whether she could get help in math from Martin without her friends' finding out. Mr. Martinson toyed with his napkin, secretly pleased with his son's ambition.

"Look!" said Mrs. Martinson. "A little surprise."

"Applesauce cake!" cried three voices in unison as they greeted its arrival on the table.

Chapter 5

Friday was always the busiest day of the week at the Glendale Fish Market. The large Roman Catholic population in the neighborhood could be counted on to buy fish that day. But, in fact, most of Glendale's housewives usually stopped by just to check out the weekly sale and take a look at the mouthwatering display in Mr. Martinson's window.

Bushel baskets of clinging purple mussels were lined up with gray coarse steamer clams that showed rubbery necks sticking out from between their hard shells. Round tubs of rough oysters and peaceful-looking cherrystone clams slept quietly on beds of rock salt, just waiting for the company of spicy tomato cocktail sauce and minced horseradish. A flow of water circulated through a glass tank, the temporary home of the blackish-green lobsters, which inched about the bottom among the shreds of seaweed, slowly waving a feeler now and again as in casual greeting. Row upon row of whole red snapper, whiting, and bluefish were meant to form a patriotic display — one of Mr. Martinson's little jokes, which no one ever got. Flat, round flounders, looking like scaly pancakes with fins, stared out at the passersby. In one corner of the window, thick slabs of coral salmon were piled in a stack, in constrast to the neat lines of freshly skinned and boned fillets. Haddock, cod, and sole, in varying shades of white and gray, waited to be dipped in breadcrumbs on their way to the frying pan. In another corner, soft cubes of scallops and coils of boiled pink shrimp perfumed the entrance to the shop with their pungent ocean aroma.

This Friday, the arrival of a large catch of swordfish had caused a big reduction in its price. Mr. Martinson and his helper, Old Frank, had their hands full keeping up with the jangling of the bell over the door and the ringing of the telephone.

"Glendale Fish Market. Oh, hi, Dolly. Welcome back. Just got your card. Some piece of Danish pastry that was! Now, what can I help you with, Dolly? How about some nice swordfish steaks, special today. Well, they're about as fresh as I am, isn't that fresh enough? Fine. I'll cut off two nice ones for you. Oh, that's no problem. No, I know there's no regular delivery, but you're special. That's what I keep telling you. Besides, my boy, Martin, will be in after school today and I'll have him drop them off on his way home. No trouble at all. Right, Dolly. You come

41

in and say 'Hi' real soon now, OK? 'Bye." Mr. Martinson put down the receiver and went back to the cutting board.

Outside, in the late afternoon sun, Martin made his way to the Shirley Street store as he did every Friday. He picked up his allowance and usually helped out for the rest of the day by sweeping up and doing odd jobs for his father. As he walked along, he could think of nothing but the two biggest events in his life right then — the change in math class and the election. Right after his mother had met with the principal, things had really started to happen.

First was the decision to make the math class change immediately. On Wednesday, he turned up as directed in the ninth-grade section to which he had been assigned.

"Since you are joining us four weeks after we have begun," his new teacher, Mrs. McManus, stated, neatly arranging a large stack of arithmetic paper, "I will see you after class with a list of additional assignments. This work should enable you to catch up with the group. Now you may take your seat."

An undercurrent of groans followed her announcement and a few sly winks indicated that he was being welcomed as a fellow sufferer rather than an enemy or an intruder. This support gave him enough confidence to let out a soft moan of his own as he sat down. For a moment he really did feel like a victim of circumstances, but one who could take the punishment.

By lunch time he was ready to accept the condolences of his friends in the seventh grade.

"I hear she gives double, two pages a night. That's ten pages of problems a week, Martin," said Howie Harris, crunching his "Sliced Vienna Roast with Bordelaise Sauce," commonly called "Mystery Meat in Its Own Blood."

"Yeah," agreed Lester, "and if you fall behind, she gives you extra work over weekends."

"Poor Martin," added little Linda Luongo, a dark-eyed, dark-haired serious girl. "You have your work cut out for you. But you'll be able to do it. You're really smart. Marty-Smarty, that's you. Marty-Smarty."

The mouth full of mayonnaise and sliced eggs across the table belonging to Marilyn Tracey picked it up and intoned, "Marty-Smarty, Marty-Smarty, that's great."

"Marty-Smarty, Marty-Smarty, Smarty-Marty," giggled silly Lucy Evans. Soon it became a chant and the entire table was tapping spoons or cups and repeating over and over, "Marty-Smarty, Marty-Smarty, MartySmartyMartySmartyMartySmarty. . . ."

The start of a laugh caught in his throat. He was embarrassed. He felt ashamed, and he didn't quite know why. But he knew he mustn't show it. What could he say without stumbling on the words? How could he stop them?

Suddenly, on an impulse, he stood up and, with

43

mock-heroic gestures, he made a sweeping bow, waving an imaginary plumed helmet. He sat down, with a bright red face, as a cafeteria monitor stormed over to quiet the disturbance, which had luckily turned to applause.

Emptying his tray a few minutes later, Martin bumped into two classmates from nearby tables. They greeted him laughingly with "See you later, Smarty," and "How're you doing in math class, Marty-Smarty?"

Lester, already behaving like a campaign manager, was unsure of the effect of this attention. He asked bluntly as they walked to their English class after lunch, "Gee, Martin, I wonder if that name will catch on? Normie Sands will sure try to use it if it works against you. He's trying to campaign before anyone else has signed up."

"I know, Lester, and believe me, it wasn't my idea, that name. You saw how it just happened. Look, it can only harm me if I hide from it. Why should I be ashamed if I am smart? Let 'em call me names. Sticks and stones, right? At least that's one way they'll remember me . . . and maybe even vote for me, too, huh?"

But as he rounded the corner toward the Glendale Fish Market, he toyed with possible slogans that wouldn't use the word *smart* in them.

"Join the winning party; cast your vote for Marty!" No, that would just remind everyone about Normie Sands's potential.

"Martin Martinson, he's our man; if he can't do it, no one can." Nope. That one was just too long. Besides, it was a football team slogan, and seventh-graders weren't allowed to be on the junior high varsity team. All they could do was play squad games. Which few came to watch. And certainly no one cheered.

Too bad he didn't have a sports-type nickname, like "Slugger" or "Killer." Well, if he won . . . no, *when* he won the election, there's only one name they would call him: "Mr. President." Or, maybe he would adopt a practice of kings or emperors. "Your Majesty" or "Your Highness" might be too strong. But, what about "Your Excellency" for a title? After all, it would only be telling the truth.

"What do you think?" he asked the big codfish that stared at him with glassy eyes, as he walked into the store and set the bell jangling.

"Oh-oh, here comes trouble now," called Old Frank. He had worked with Martin's grandfather in the old days in the wholesale market and had known the boy since the day he was born. Although Old Frank was supposed to be retired, he liked to keep busy. So on Fridays, when some help was needed, he worked alongside Mr. Martinson, putting in a good full day's work.

"Not if you don't ask for it," answered Martin, putting up his fists as he always did. They had a running joke that one day the young boy was going to be so strong he'd be able to lick Old Frank. In truth, they were very close friends, despite the difference in age, and would never lay a finger on one another, even in jest.

"If you two prizefighters can lay down the gloves for a minute, I can use some help. Martin, will you get the broom and sweep up some of this mess back here? Then put down some more sawdust. You know where it is."

They retired to imaginary neutral corners. Martin put on a white apron folded in half to keep from dragging on the floor, and within minutes was busy working away, tidying up and cleaning as a steady ringing of the doorbell tolled business as usual.

Around 4:30 that afternoon, Mr. Martinson told him to take off the apron and to put on his cap and jacket.

"It's early, Dad. I don't have to leave yet."

"No, Martin, I have a special delivery for you to make and it's a little out of the way, so I think you'd better start off now. Here's a package I want you to take up to Mrs. Sutter, Dolly Sutter, over on Alden Terrace, up in the Heights. That's a good walk, so you'd better get going. If she wants to pay you, here's change for a ten-dollar bill. If she doesn't, that's OK, too. She's a good customer. The slip's in the bag. Take your time, but don't lollygag on your way over there. I'll see you at supper."

46

Martin sighed. The Heights. That was a good half-hour walk, even for him. It wasn't really even in Glendale, but there were no stores out that way. People who lived there had to do their shopping in Glendale or go all the way into town. Well, the walk would give him some more time to think about the election.

The Sutter house didn't look big on the outside. It was set back behind a small lawn with a few strange, twisted trees, which cast dark, mysterious shadows in the chill autumn twilight. But the house went on and on toward the back, where it opened onto a huge yard, which in turn merged into something that looked like a forest. Martin could hardly see the end of it as he stood at the back door and waited for the doorbell to be answered.

A pleasant, thin woman, with dark hair streaked by blonde and gray patches, opened the door. At the same time she was talking to someone in another room.

"I have it, Hattie, I have it. You go on home now and take care of that sniffle. Come in, dear," she said to Martin. "It's raw outside."

"That's OK, ma'am," said Martin. "I have your package here. From Martinson's. The Glendale Fish Market."

"Oh, that's wonderful. But you come right in here

and sit down and warm up a bit. It's getting awfully cold now, or it seems like it is since the days are growing shorter. You must be the Martinson boy, aren't you?"

"Yes, ma'am," he replied. "I'm Martin."

"Well, Martin, I've been doing business with your father a long time and we're practically old friends by now. I wouldn't feel right if I didn't give his son something to warm him up before he headed off into this cold evening. I'm going to have some tea myself, but I'm going to make you drink a cup of hot chocolate before you go. Now just take off your jacket and sit right there," she said, indicating a wrought-iron chair covered with pink plastic, next to a round table. Martin thought it looked just like the ones at Bregmann's Ice Cream Shoppe.

She opened up a covered tin that had pictures of pink and blue white-haired ladies all over it and took out several thin cookies iced on one side with chocolate.

"Here, these aren't home-made, but they come from Denmark. Try one now, you can have more with your cocoa."

In no time at all, they were sitting at the little round table. She was sipping tea and he was trying not to gulp or make noise as he nibbled on the cookies and drank the hot chocolate. Mrs. Sutter talked practically nonstop at first, but eventually Martin warmed

48

up. He began to catch her little pause for breath which gave him an opportunity to answer, or even make comments of his own. Before long they were chatting away quite amiably.

Mrs. Sutter told him that she and Mr. Sutter had lived in the Heights house for almost fifteen years. They had two grown sons who were married and lived in Chicago, where one was a doctor, and California, where the other was a lawyer. They also had a daughter, who was away in college.

Martin asked, "What is she studying? I mean, what's she going to be when she graduates?"

"An Indian chief!" Mrs. Sutter replied and burst out laughing. "I'm sorry, but that happens all the time. Actually she's majoring in education and wants to teach elementary school. You're beyond that by now, aren't you?" she asked.

"Oh, yes, I'm in the seventh grade."

"Do you like it?"

"It's all right."

"Oh, what's your favorite subject?"

"Mmmmm . . . well, I don't really have a favorite. Well, yes, I do. It's English. I like it now because it's mostly reading, not just learning the parts of speech and all that anymore."

"I'm so glad to hear that," said Mrs. Sutter as she poured some more hot chocolate into his mug. "I loved studying English. I concentrated in literature

49

when I was in teacher's college. Of course, it wasn't a regular university like today's. When I went off to study, we had what they called Normal Schools where you trained specifically to become a teacher. Oh, we had classes in so many things I thought were silly, like how high to raise the windows in class-rooms. And how to write neatly on the blackboard. Blackboard penmanship, indeed! But, I was mostly interested in reading and I planned to teach English literature when I graduated."

"Did you?" asked Martin.

"Did I what? Oh, did I teach English? No, I graduated on a Tuesday and I married Mr. Sutter the following Sunday. And I never went to work. But I did have my love of literature and reading as a life-long legacy from my schooldays. Even now I still study certain areas of literature. And once in a while I write a little article for one of those magazines which nobody ever really reads. Would you like to know what I'm working on now?"

"Sure," said Martin.

"I'm writing an article on William Shakespeare and his tragic heroes."

"Wow, that's what we're reading! I mean, not a whole play, just some speeches. My sister's class is reading *Julius Caesar* and I've started that, too. I already know that Caesar's not the real hero of the play; Brutus is."

"Well, you're one step in the right direction. And I'm delighted to hear that the schools haven't dropped Shakespeare from the curriculum. So many things are out of fashion these days. But, my heavens, look at the time. We've been gabbing away for almost an hour. Your mother will be worried about you."

"I'd better be going, Mrs. Sutter. Gee, thanks for the cocoa and the cookies. And it sure was swell talking to you. Thanks, thanks for everything."

"You run along now, Martin. I'll telephone your home and tell them you're on your way."

Martin recited his telephone number, which she wrote down on a small notepad while he zipped up his jacket.

"Fine, I'll explain to your mother that I filled you with chocolate and idle conversation."

"Oh, no, I really enjoyed it, I mean, talking about school and everything, and the cocoa, too."

Mrs. Sutter's face turned pink and rosy and her eyes became shiny, too, as she touched his shoulder.

"This has been a very happy hour for me, too. And we'll talk some more in the future. Now, you'd better be off."

She leaned down and gave him the slightest peck of a kiss on his cheek. Martin flushed, opened the door, and sped off.

It was only a moment after he left that it dawned

on him. He hadn't received the usual nickel or dime, or even quarter, he counted on when he made deliveries for his father.

Yeah, but it was worth it. That was the best delivery I ever made, he thought. Mrs. Sutter is special. And talking with her is worth more than any two bits. Or even double.

Chapter 6

"The meeting will now come to order!"

There were six of them gathered in Lester Lerner's bedroom that Saturday morning. And the call to order had been sounded three times already when Lester, determined to get their attention, shouted one last time, "All right, you guys, let's have some order or I'm taking back my comic books and everything else and you'll have to leave."

That seemed to penetrate. One by one they grudgingly stopped their reading, conversations, and playful jabbing at one another. Seats were found on the twin beds, on the desk chair, and on the floor as they focused their attention on the slight form and loud voice of their host.

"All right, OK, we're gonna run this meeting according to the rules of order. That means, no talking while someone else is. Now, we start off with a roll call. When I say your name, answer 'Here'; got it?" announced Lester.

"I don't see what the big deal about *order* is," said Bobby Newsome. Next to Lester he was the smallest person in the room, but he had a shrill, high-pitched voice and could always get attention when he wanted to by using it.

" 'Cause if we don't have a little order," said Bernie Williams, who lived in the same apartment house as Bobby, "nobody will get in a word, 'cept for you." And he reached over to the other twin bed and gave his sometimes best friend a little jab in the chest. Bobby was about to poke him back, but was held off by Martin.

"Hey, guys, come on. No fooling around. We gotta get started or we'll never get anywhere. We all agreed to come here and let Lester run things. Right? So let's cut out the dumb stuff and get down to business. We know who's here, Lester. Just mark down the names of everyone in the room — you, me, Bobby, Bernie, Howie, and Stevie. 'The Crest Street Gang,' " he said and set off a roar of snickers and howls at the suggestion that they were in the same category as Dillinger, Al Capone, and Ma Barker and her boys.

The last two names called off belonged to Martin's friends of long standing who didn't exactly live on Crest Street but had close ties to it. Howie Harris had lived in number 27, across the street from Bobby and Bernie, until a year ago, when his parents moved the family to a larger apartment around the corner. Stevie Phillips actually lived a block away, above a linoleum store at the edge of the business district. But both his parents worked and he grew up spending most of his time at his grandparents' house right on the corner of Crest Street.

"All right, most of us know why we're here this morning, but in case anyone doesn't, I might as well tell you. Our friend, and in most cases, neighbor —"

"Wait a minute," said Stevie, "just 'cause I don't live here don't mean I'm not as close to Martin as you guys!"

"Nobody said you weren't, Stevie. Keep your lid on," shouted Bobby.

"Anyhow," Lester continued, "our pal, Martin, has decided to run for class president of the seventh grade at Taft Junior High School."

"Hooray!"

"Wahoo . . . let's hear it for ol' Martin."

"Attago, pal, go, Martin!"

"Thanks, fellas," said Martin. "But it's going to take a lot more than just your votes to win the election. You know what's going on as well as I do. Even though nobody's officially put their name in, Normie Sands has let everyone know that he's running. And he's starting to promise a lot of things if he gets elected."

"Yeah, I hear he's already talking about a big victory party when he wins," said Bernie.

"Big deal," said Bobby. "Who wants to go to one of his old parties, anyhow?"

"You would," said Bernie, "if you ever got invited."

"Yeah, but who'd ever invite someone ugly as you?" added Howie. "Besides, you'd eat all the potato chips, drink a gallon of Coke, and then get sick, like you did at the beach last summer."

"Aw, nuts to you," muttered Bobby.

"Yeah, well, the big problem is that a lot of kids just look at those parties as the only reason to vote for someone," said Lester. "We've got to come up with some reasons why people should vote for more than that, for someone who knows what he's doing, like Martin."

"OK, OK, we all know that and we all think Martin's an OK guy, 'cause he's our friend, and we know him," said Stevie, scratching his nose.

"And we know that just 'cause he's smart doesn't mean he's not a regular guy," added Bobby. "But this 'Marty-Smarty' stuff doesn't help. We just have to find a way to show everyone else that he's more than just another smart guy."

Bernie asked, "Do you suppose you could just walk around acting dumb, you know, walking into telephone poles, like Bobby here? Huh, Martin?"

"Don't be so wise," blurted Bobby. Martin clenched his lips to keep from smiling at the reminder of the shiner Bobby had gotten a week ago from doing just that.

"I thought of it," he said, "but I don't think it would work. I'm not good at faking, and if I got caught, it would be worse than anything. Besides, how many times do we get told 'You have a brain?

Well, use it!' I know my mother says it about ten times a week to me and Helena."

"*Helena and me,*" yelled Bobby. "Hey, I caught the genius already. See, he ain't so smart after all. Hey, I'm smarter than Martin. Everybody, hear that. Wow!" and he slid off the bed on to the floor in a fit of mock hysteria.

"Maybe that's an approach. We go around and show how, in some way, everyone's a little smarter than Martin. So he's just an ordinary guy like everyone else. Whattaya think of that?"

"That still doesn't give any reason to vote *for* him, only not against him. You know what I mean?" asked Lester. "I think it's time we heard from the candidate."

Spontaneous applause, whistles, and a few shouts came from the young bodies scattered about. Everyone turned toward Martin.

"All right, fellas, I'm not going to make a big speech for you guys. Besides, you wouldn't let me. You'd just keep butting in. 'Specially Bobby, since he's an authority on grammar now."

"Hear, hear."

"I'll tell you what I've been thinking about and then you tell me what you think about it and then maybe we can get it across to everyone else in the class. All right? OK, here goes. I figure . . ."

Voices were lowered. The soft chenille bedspreads, the scatter rugs on the floor, the collection of coats and caps on the maple clothes pole, all closed in and muffled the sound of their whispers. Lester Lerner's bedroom was transformed into a chamber of conspirators as the small, dedicated band of friends joined together to plan the strategy and plot the political campaign that they hoped would lead to the election of their pal, Martin.

The Sunday paper was scattered about the living room. Martin, stretched out on the couch, leaned on his elbows and mumbled a running commentary on the sports section, while Helena carefully studied the rotogravure and weekly magazine. Every once in a while, she would raise her eyebrows and exclaim, "Well, I like that!" or "Wouldn't you just know!" as she discovered items of interest about her favorite celebrities or startling shifts in the world of fashions.
The Martinson children had the newspaper and the living room to themselves. Mrs. Martinson was busy in the kitchen while her husband was lost at his desk in the bedroom going through the stack of bookkeeping papers. The door was shut and he could not hear the strains of lush music that swept through the house as the kitchen radio poured out the songs of Victor Herbert, Rodgers and Hammerstein, Jerome Kern, and other "light classics" interpreted by popular orchestras with huge violin sections. Once in a while a sweet, husky soprano or a mellow-sounding male voice would croon the lyrics to a popular tune of the day and Helena or Martin would drift into the song.

"You made me love you, yumpy-dumpy-dum-dum," hummed Helena as she listlessly turned the pages.

"What did you find, a picture of you-know-who in the paper? You'd stand a better chance in the sports section," said Martin.

"Don't be so fresh, Mr. Marty-Smarty," snapped Helena toward the direction of the couch. The absence of a quick reply caused her to turn and look at her brother before he could hide his flushed face.

"I'm sorry, Mart, I shouldn't have done that. I shouldn't have said it. And you know I didn't mean to be . . . well, *mean.* I heard about what happened in the cafeteria and I'm proud of you for standing up and taking it. That was really neat, the way you handled it."

"Thanks. It's OK. It wasn't so bad."

"Listen, you know how Dad said that we'd all help with the election if you want. You know, I really will if you want me to do something. I don't guess I know anyone in your class that you don't know better, but I could talk to some of my friends if you want. They might know some kids in your class. Gloria Simmons's cousin is in it, I think."

"Hey, that would be terrific, and who knows, it might help. But, boy, we've got a lot of work to do, campaigning and everything. And on top of that, I've got all this math homework to do now. I ought to be doing that before dinner, so I can work on the election stuff later."

"I'd help you, but you can probably do the math better and quicker than I can. Besides, Mr. Saraceno is a lot different from Mrs. McManus, and we might get confused trying to do it together. But, Martin," she purred, "maybe you ought to get someone in your math class to work on the problems with you. Someone who could probably use a little help from you, too."

"Someone like a football player named Rick Petersen?" smiled Martin.

"Oh, Martin, if you got him over here to work on math, I'd do anything you asked. I'd make your bed, take out the garbage, do the dishes. I'd even walk up and down in front of the school begging for kids to vote for you!" Helena's words came out so fast she didn't seem to realize the promises she was making. Luckily, Martin didn't take her seriously.

"Hey, I'm not going to guarantee anything," he said, "but if I even get a chance to talk to him, I'll sort of let that Rick Petersen know that there's help available here in math. And if he finds out that I have a beautiful sister, he might just take me up on my offer."

"Martin, when was the last time I squeezed you and kissed you so hard you couldn't breathe?"

"Help! Help! There's a crazy-lady after me!" He threw a fringed pillow at her, and began to laugh.

The two matching bedroom lamps with the white ruffled shades lighted the opposite corners of the big double bed in the Martinsons' bedroom. Curled up in his corner, Mr. Martinson was reading the real estate section of the Sunday newspaper; Mrs. Martinson, her eyeglasses resting on the tip of her nose, was propped up on her pillows, cutting coupons from a magazine.

"Stanley," she said quietly.

"Hmmmm?"

"Stanley, I've been thinking about that election."

"What are you thinking about it?"

"I just don't know whether it's such a good idea," she replied.

"You'd rather the school went Communist? Did away with elections like the Reds?"

"Don't be funny. You know what I'm talking about. I'm just not so sure about Martin running for president. He could be asking for a lot more trouble than he thinks. And keep your voice down."

Now sitting up, Mr. Martinson said, "I get it. You think he's too *sensitive*, that he'll be *hurt* if he loses. . . ."

"*When* he loses," she interrupted. "That Sands boy is the most popular kid in his class, if not the school."

"Now, don't be so sure that it's in the bag. Remember the last presidential election. Tom Dewey thought he had that one all sewn up. Besides, Martin is a lot stronger; he's got a more mature character than you give him credit for. And let's not overlook the fact that the boy is just plain smart. Intelligent. That counts for something. Oh, I know you don't think

61

that all his knowledge, that memory and his way with numbers, are much help in everyday life. But you just watch out. That boy will come up with something."

"Have you watched him lately, I mean without looking directly at him?" She smiled. "I can tell the way his eyes flicker about a thousand times a minute. Oh, that brain is working away, all right. You have something there. But will that be enough?"

Mr. Martinson folded the newspaper and put it on the night table next to the lamp. He switched off the light and slid down under the blankets.

"It'll be whatever it will be," he mumbled. "Now, let's get some sleep. Martin's old enough to take care of himself at school. Stop babying him."

Mrs. Martinson put away her scissors and shut off her lamp, too. She leaned over and tapped Mr. Martinson playfully, gently on the shoulder. No response. She scrutinized the wrinkled blanket and found her mark, just below the shoulder and a little to the left. Firm knuckles ground in and rubbed, doing their work on his most ticklish spot.

"Help!" he whispered. "There's a crazy-lady after me!"

Chapter 7

By Tuesday, Martin had rounded up the twenty signatures he needed to file his nomination papers for the presidency of his class. He brought them to the administrative office at the close of school that day.

"Do I just leave them here, or do I get a receipt or anything?" he asked Miss Bellini.

Not looking half so fierce as she had looked the last time he visited that office, she smiled and asked him to wait a minute.

"I'll just fill your name in on this certificate of nomination. For the record. And you can have this carbon copy," she said.

He had sat down on the shiny oak bench next to the teachers' mailboxes when the principal's door opened and Mr. Lindstrom walked out to hand some folders to Miss Bellini. As he turned to go back in his office, he noticed Martin sitting there.

"Well, Martinson," he said. "Not here for detention, I hope."

"No, sir," Martin replied. "I'm waiting for my nomination certificate. I'm running for class office, for president."

"Hm, with your . . . uh . . . capacity, you ought to do well. I'll have to keep an eye on this election and see what the polls say as it gets closer," he chuckled. Then he entered his office and closed the door crisply behind him, his chins still rippling with amusement.

It figures, thought Martin. He *would* believe in polls.

By the next day, the whole seventh grade knew just about everything there was to know about the election. "Everything" included the names of those who were seeking the offices of president, vice-president, secretary, and treasurer. These were spoken of casually but constantly. Still, no real issues had come up. One certifiable fact was clear: if Normie Sands were elected, there would be the biggest celebration, the best party anyone could ever imagine. Other than that, no one seemed to have much to say about the various candidates.

Bobby Newsome and Bernie Williams were throwing a football back and forth on one side of the playing field right after school on Thursday. It was just before official team practice started, while most of the kids were drifting off home. They had the area pretty much to themselves. Bobby came back panting after chasing a long ball he had missed and called it quits. He and Bernie started walking off together.

"Whaddya think of Martin's chances?" he asked when he had caught his breath.

"Bobby, how do I know? I mean, we think he's a terrific guy and all that, but I just don't know whether this idea he has is so red hot."

"But you're gonna go through with it on Monday, huh? You're not going to chicken out, are you?"

Bernie replied, "No way. I said I would and I will. But I'll be glad when it's over. Sometimes school's a real pain, if you know what I mean."

"Hey, Bernie, catch this," said Bobby and he flipped the ball in a wobbly lateral pass. "You're just still sore 'cause the Giants lost last Sunday. You should play for them. You're as bad as they are. Whoo! Whoo!"

It seemed to him that all the little steamer clams were sticking out their tongues as Martin walked by the bushel baskets sitting on the bed of ice at the front of the store.

"Nyah, nyah, yourselves," he said to them as he put his hat on the peg and started to take off his coat.

"Wait a minute, Martin," said his father. "We have a change in signals today."

"Yep," chuckled Old Frank, "young fella's got a secret admirer, that's what."

"Pipe down, old-timer," said Mr. Martinson. "Let me tell him the story before you go on . . . uh . . .

interrupting it. Martin, Dolly Sutter called and asked me if you could deliever some fish to her today. And, she asked if I minded if you came by a little earlier so she could have a little talk with you. Dolly said you were a very nice, polite young man and she enjoyed your interest in Shakespeare."

"Really? Gee, I didn't, I mean, gee . . ."

"Martin, Dolly is a very clever woman. She writes serious articles about Shakespeare for some important magazines. Listening to her could do you some good. Here's the package for her. Now, mind your manners and don't eat every single thing Dolly offers you. If I know Dolly, it'll be some kind of special cake or cookies. And it'll be awfully good."

"But what about the store? Who's going to do the sweeping and everything?"

"It's a little slow this week. I think Old Frank and I can handle things today. Don't you worry, there'll be plenty of sawdust for you to toss around next week. You just get started and have a nice time at Dolly's. And behave yourself."

Martin flipped the package back and forth, right to left hand and back. It wasn't very heavy, but lumpy and sort of soft for its bulk. Careful, he remembered, got to make sure not to toss it too hard and tear the paper bag. Next thing you know, it would start leaking and the fish smell would ooze out. Probably have a million cats following me, he chuckled to himself.

He was halfway up the hill toward Mrs. Sutter's house when he decided to take a little detour. Normie Sands lived nearby. Even though he'd gone by before, Martin had never really taken a good look at the Sands house. Besides being a good place for parties, was there anything so great about it? He was curious. And it wouldn't take that long.

He turned left, walked about a hundred steps and saw the sign, "Walnut Place, Private Way." Well, it ran between Thornwood and Highdale, didn't it? If you wanted to get to one of those streets, you had to go through Walnut Place, unless you wanted to walk about a mile out of the way, didn't you? So who's going to know that he didn't really have to get to Thornwood Street or Highdale Road anyhow, he figured.

About halfway down the block stood the Sands house, set back behind a beautiful, rich green lawn without a single leaf on it. They must have someone come out and pick up the leaves every fifteen minutes, Martin thought to himself as he slowed down in front of the house.

Staring straight ahead and lost in thought, Martin didn't see or hear the side door open as Normie Sands came outside, shouting back at a little girl who followed him.

"Why do you have to tag along everywhere I go? For cryin' out loud, don't you have any friends of your own? Cheez, Melissa, what a pain you are!"

The little girl scowled and paid no attention as she followed at his heels, carrying a large basket of worn-out tennis balls.

Normie saw Martin a second before Martin saw him. A look of black rage crossed his features before he turned it to an obviously forced smile and said, "Well, what brings you here, Martinson?"

Startled, Martin replied, "I . . . uh . . . I was just on my way to Thornwood Street with this package. I didn't know you lived here, I mean right in this house. I mean . . . I never noticed the house before."

"Well, if you're really on your way to Thorn-wood . . . if you *really* are . . . you must be in a hurry to come through Walnut Place. It is a *private* street, you know."

"OK, there's a sign that says it's private, but there aren't any gates or chains across the road, you know. Like over at Phelps Terrace or Hawthorne Way."

"Oh, yeah? Well, it's private just the same. And the sign is supposed to keep people like you out," Normie snarled.

"It does, does it?" replied Martin, glaring at him. "Well, what are you going to do about it?"

The two boys were standing about six feet apart, feet firm on the ground, leaning in toward each other. Martin was ready to drop the package and start swinging. He hadn't been in a real fistfight in years, but he never forgot what Old Frank had once told him: get in the first punch. That was the most important thing. One more smart-alecky word from Normie, and he was ready to deliver.

Melissa hadn't paid much attention to the boys. She had heard this type of talk before and wasn't very interested in it. Instead, she had scattered the tennis balls on the lawn and was skipping about them, singing to herself. As their talk grew fiercer, she danced close to the edge of the lawn and kicked one of the balls into the street. She started to chase the ball, running behind Martin as a big sedan came down the street and headed for the bouncing object.

It looked for one second as though the girl would go crashing into the car, but Martin caught the action from the corner of his eye and instinctively reached out just in time to grab her by the sleeve.

It was exactly at that moment that Normie Sands advanced and swung at Martin. But Martin's gesture pulled him out of the reach of Normie's arm, and Normie missed completely.

The car screeched to a halt and the driver leaned out the window and started shouting, "Keep those kids off the street, for Pete's sake!"

Melissa had begun to cry, more from the knowledge that she had misbehaved than from any real hurt. Martin gave her a pat on her arm and picked up the tennis ball, which had rolled back to their side of the street. He tossed it away up on the lawn as the window in front of them opened and Mrs. Sands yelled out.

"I told you to keep an eye on her. How many times do I have to remind you? I have a good mind not to take you two out to dinner tonight. Now, don't let me hear another thing from either of you!"

Slam. Down went the window and the little girl, still crying, ran into the house. Normie shrugged his shoulders and turned away from Martin. Without a word, he followed her inside.

As he headed down the street, Martin realized that he was soaking wet under his jacket. He was tired and buoyant, angry and happy, all at the same time. He had stood up to Normie Sands and, as far as he was concerned, he had won the first big round.

Chapter 8

A few trees still stood on Crest Street. At one time, graceful elms, maples, honey locust, and an occasional oak had lined both sides, growing out of the patches of green that stood between the cement sidewalks and the macadam road. But, as the neighborhood changed, most of the trees had given way to storms, pollution — or just old age. Now the grassy plots were gone, the sidewalks completely paved. The few remaining trees stood out among the intruders: rows of creosote-soaked utility poles and squat red and yellow fire hydrants.

The old horse chestnut tree near the corner had seen better days, but it held on valiantly. A bitter winter with raging snowstorms followed by freezing rain had cost it several major limbs. Still, it had managed to put out leaves last spring and earlier in the fall it had dropped the round, spiky balls that, when opened, yielded shiny brown horse chestnuts. They were no good for eating, everyone knew. And since there were no horses around anymore, they weren't needed for fodder. If, indeed, horses ever ate them! No one knew. Despite all that, the lustrous, smooth nuggets had the tempting appeal of discovered treasure, and they were highly prized as useful ammunition in the arsenal of street fighting.

Since serious weaponry that could cause real harm — slingshots, peashooters, big rocks, glass, or metal — was banned by general consent of all the neighborhood kids and enforced by all their mothers, horse chestnuts just squeaked under the thin line of "acceptable."

Stockpiling was common. The waxy horse chestnuts were gathered and stored in jars and tin cans that had once held collections of marbles. When one youngster had enough, or when he joined with another or a group, "war" could be declared. A respectable amount of space between combatants was generally agreed upon and then the missiles flew. Back and forth. Strike. Miss. Pow. A hit, a good, solid zonk on the old noggin was the best that could be hoped for. It might even produce a small black-and-blue mark. But mostly the chestnuts fell wide of the mark and were retrieved and thrown back. The battle continued until almost all the ammunition had disappeared in bushes, down sewers, or under parked cars. Or, just as likely, the armies grew tired of the game and began to yell at each other, call for an armistice, put down the chestnuts, and retire from the field of battle. A serious breach of street warfare etiquette, the approach of night, an urgent need to use the bathroom, or any one of several acceptable reasons would result in a quickly negotiated truce.

"Wait until next time," said Stevie to Howie as they sat under the old chestnut tree. While he spoke, he nested and carefully folded a gigantic horse chestnut into a handkerchief and then bound it with a rubber band.

"What're you going to do," asked Howie, "pull a sneak attack? What's that going to accomplish? Knock off one guy!"

"Naw, I'll save it for an over-the-hill assault, like that movie we saw Saturday."

"I don't think we're gonna have another war for a while. 'Sides, pretty soon it'll snow and we can have snowball fights."

Stevie thought for a minute, "So then maybe I'll wrap it up inside a snowball."

Howie replied quickly, "Uh-uh, that's dirty. No fair. You could really hurt someone, maybe put out his eye. You know the rules. You gotta play fair."

"Just like Martin and this election, huh?" said Stevie.

"Yeah, like that. Play by the rules, but bend them a little to get around them. I'm really looking forward to tomorrow. Nobody expects nothin', far as I know."

"I guess everybody thinks the only thing's gonna happen for the election is the big assembly just before the voting. That's all that's ever been done. Taft is kind of cool about politics. Martin's sister says that nobody really pays that much attention usually."

"Boy, is this gonna be a surprise! But, there's nothin' in the rules says we can't do it."

"Rules," said Stevie, rubbing the cloth-covered chestnut along the side of his face. "There's always rules. Nuts!"

Chapter 9

T he next morning, Martin woke early and chose his clothes very carefully. The President of the country used to own a men's clothing store and was a very neat dresser. It was important to look right. Not too smooth. Not too sloppy. Somewhere right down the middle; that was the idea. He decided on a nice maroon plaid shirt that he thought made him look like "one of the guys" whenever he wore it.

"So when does the campaign start?" asked Helena at the breakfast table. "When do you start asking the kids to vote for you? In my class, nobody even cares about the elections, and I probably wouldn't even notice them if you weren't in one."

"That's what's happened. Taft elections are a big joke, a big popularity contest and nothing else. There almost isn't any reason to have them anymore," Martin replied. "But I've been working on that. You'll find out soon. You'll see."

"Say, don't forget I'm your sister. Anything you do, people will associate with me. So don't go wild, huh?"

"Don't worry." He went on in his best imitation Humphrey Bogart voice, "And listen, sister, I may just be able to take care of your parking tickets if you play your cards right. You know, keep you and your bike out of jail."

"You nutcake," Helena laughed. "I don't even have a bike anymore."

It was warm for that time of year. The October sun blazed down on the Taft school grounds and cast clean shadows, which created a cool patch on one side of the building as well as dark spots that stretched away from the scattered trees. On a nice day like this, the same clusters that divided up the cafeteria at lunchtime spilled outside in roughly the same groups, with some drifting taking place as homework was compared in anticipation of the afternoon classes. A certain amount of casual socializing between the sexes was considered OK, too.

The school building itself formed a giant U-shape, with a gravel yard in between the two sides. Broad steps in the middle led up to the entrance and the administrative office. On a nice day, when it was comfortable enough to spend part of the lunch period outside, those steps were considered the prime position for seeing and being seen. The best spots weren't reserved, but were usually commandeered by the "top cats." Sure enough, there was Rick Petersen over on one side, laughing and talking to a group of admirers. And the president of the dramatic club (she had been elected the year before) was flapping her arms as she made her point to a gathering of eager listeners. The Number One Gossip, who would have won by a landslide if there had been an election for that office, had the attention of half a dozen admirers, including, Martin noticed, Marilyn Tracey.

Well, this is it, he thought. He gave a signal by winking at Lester, who disappeared back into the cafeteria entrance. A few minutes later, he reappeared, followed by Bernie, Bobby, Howie, and Stevie, each of them carrying two milk crates.

Marching straight ahead, looking forward and never letting their eyes stray to one side or the other, they arrived at the bottom of the steps and dropped the crates.

The sight of the five of them forging their way through the crowd with such determination attracted some attention, some snickers, and a few catcalls.

"Here comes the clean-up squad."

"Hey, free milk for everyone, huh?"

"Don'cha know there's a law against stealing milk crates!"

Ignoring everyone, they assembled the crates into a platform smack in the middle of the area in front of the steps. Then they formed a guard around this construction as Martin climbed up to the top. He took a small cardboard megaphone, which Lester had carried in one of the crates and had handed to him as he got up on the platform.

"Hear ye, hear ye, all seventh-graders of the William Howard Taft Junior High School and anyone else who is interested in good government of the school" — a long deep breath, then — "of the students, by the students, and for the students."

It was such a strange sight, such an unusual sound to be heard in that place at that time, that nearly everyone in the area stopped. Surprised, they looked at Martin, then at each other, and then they looked at Martin again.

Thankful that he had their attention, he went on immediately in a clear, strong voice.

"There are serious issues which face students here at Taft which have been ignored for too long a time. Now there is an opportunity to do something about them. My name is Martin Martinson and I am a candidate for the office of president of the seventh-grade class here at Taft."

This announcement prompted a few scattered cries of "Boo!" from the outer sections, but they were quickly drowned out by shouts of "Hooray!" and "Hear! Hear!" most noticeably from the four corners surrounding the platform. The large group gathered in the area was beginning to expand with the addition of stragglers who started into the circle from other parts of the school grounds. Only the hardened cigarette smokers, who kept out of sight behind the bushes near the ditch, were completely out of reach of his voice.

"I would like to take this opportunity to talk to you about one important issue which faces the members of the seventh grade. It is a matter of discrimination, and I think something should be done about it. Today I will tell you what it is. And I will also tell you what I think should be done.

"It concerns — it's about tickets to Taft football games, both home games played here and away games played away. Elsewhere. I think it's a disgrace that seventh-graders are segregated into the crummiest section, the worst seats, in the end zone. We are members of the school and just as good as anyone else. Before seats are put on general sale, we should have a chance to get our seats in the sideline stands just like the eighth- and ninth-graders."

By now, some of the crowd realized that this was a speech primarily for the seventh grade, and probably not of interest to a lot of them. So some had started up their own private conversations as Martin went on. This caused him to raise his voice, even with the megaphone, so that he was practically shouting every word.

"I promise you that if I am elected, I will do something about it. There are ways to change things and I will take this up with the . . . the administration. And, as a class, we can all take whatever steps are necessary to correct this terrible situation.

"This is just the first of many things I will do if I

am elected. There are lots of others. Watch for future announcements by the Martinson for President Campaign Committee, who are gathered here," and he nodded at the crate-bearers who still surrounded the platform. "We will be coming to you from now on, asking you to vote with your head, to think before you vote. Thank you for your attention, thank you very much."

When he stopped, the milk-crate quintet started up a repetitive chant, "Martinson — president — Martinson — president," sounding very much like a steam locomotive. They were joined by strays in the crowd who were amused, who liked the courage of the boy who dared to get up in the middle of the dull lunchtime gathering, or who were simply swept up by the seductive rhythm of the chant.

The candidate was now off the platform, circulating and shaking hands with some classmates, even getting a sly wink from Marilyn Tracey, when his ears picked up a different tune coming from another corner.

"Marty-Smarty, Marty-Smarty, Marty-Smarty," mocked a small but boisterous band of followers gathered around Normie Sands. The object of their derision had seen Normie's eyes almost bulge out of their sockets when he had begun his speech. But his concentration on winning over the crowd and keeping their attention had been so intense, he had lost sight of the opposition. He hadn't noticed Normie rounding up his loyal gang, and their response caught him unawares. He looked around for Lester, for Bernie, Howie, and the others to urge them to shout louder, even if it turned the normally quiet lunch period into a shouting contest, but his followers were spread out. Normie was heading for the milk-crate platform, which still stood in the center, and was about to try to take over when, just as it happened in the movies, the bell rang and they all had to return to their classes. The crowd began to file into the various entrances, the smokers came out of the bushes, and the milk crates were gathered up by Martin's group.

As he grabbed his two cases, Lester said to Howie, "Boy, that's what you really call 'saved by the bell,' huh?"

Martin, who had joined them to help out, heard Lester's remarks and said, "Yeah, I don't care what anyone says; I think it was a good start. You just watch."

"Uh huh," said Bobby, "I'll bet half those kids didn't even know you were alive before, Martin. Some of them thought you were just an A-plus in history or something. Now, they'll know you are a person."

"Yeah," laughed Bernie. "With a big mouth."

"Well," said Martin, clearing his throat, which had started to become hoarse, "I guess it was a little more than that. I hope it started some of 'em thinking a little, too. Who knows? At least, right now. C'mon, we've gotta get in before we're late. See what you hear this afternoon and let's get together after supper. I told my mom we're having a meeting in my room tonight."

"What's the matter with my house? I thought that was campaign headquarters," asked Lester.

"We're afraid you'll charge us rent," said Stevie. "Besides, we've read all your comic books. Let's see what Martin has to offer."

Helena had been talking to her two best friends, Nancy Robbins and Inez McMullin, when the sound of her brother's muffled and amplified voice cut through the general buzz in the schoolyard. She could hardly believe her ears. Martin, her kid brother, braving the crowd, standing up on a soapbox — no, those were milk crates — making a political speech. Then, in a flash, she was embarrassed. She started to move closer, to hear better, followed right at her heels by Nancy and Inez. She started to blush, but then she noticed that the kids were really listening to him and he didn't sound half bad. Of course, who really cared what he was saying; it was more important that they paid attention. And showed respect. Maybe he did have a chance of winning.

The three girls edged their way closer, but they didn't want to get mixed up with the seventh-graders, who were right near the makeshift platform. Instead, they made a wide swing to one side and gradually climbed the steps so that they could watch from above. Her eyes fixed on the figure talking into the megaphone, Helena put her foot down short of one step and caught her heel. She had started slipping forward when a strong arm reached out and grabbed her by the elbow, steadying her and preventing a fall.

"Careful there," said a low, pleasant voice, "you're liable to end up in the candidate's lap."

"It's usually the other way around. Or at least it used to be. I'm his sister," said Helena, staring directly into the deep blue eyes of Rick Petersen.

"Very good," he laughed. "You should be proud of him. It takes guts to get up in front of a crowd. That's right, you're Helena Martinson. Funny, I didn't put the two of you together when he came into my math class."

"Well, we don't look much alike, but we're very close," said Helena, trying to forget the millions of times she had wished she were an only child. She went on, "Thank you for catching me before I tumbled."

"Glad to be of assistance. I might even call on you if I need some help. Wish I were as good in math as your brother. Does it run in the family?"

"Hardly!" she laughed. "But I'll tell you what, as a sign of my appreciation, I hereby offer my brother's services. He can do you more good there than I can."

"I don't know about that, but I might just have to accept the offer. I'm not the greatest with numbers. But you and Martin don't owe me anything. So, if he does end up helping me with math, maybe I can give him a hand with this election. Although he doesn't sound like he needs any help. So far. Hey, see you around." And he climbed down the steps. Martin's speech had now ended, and the chanting had begun. Helena could hardly hear Nancy and Inez, who were pressing up against her and feverishly asking, "What did he say? What did you say? What did he say, then?"

It had happened so fast and casually that Helena could hardly believe it had really taken place. In no time at all she had gotten closer to Rick without all the scheming she thought it would take. Still, where exactly was she? Well, they were on better speaking terms, even familiar. And now all she had to do was hope that he would have trouble in math. Or that Martin would have trouble with the election.

Just then, she heard the shouts of "Marty-Smarty, Marty-Smarty" starting up. Her first impulse was to go over and smack those wise guys. On second thought — well, it seemed disloyal, but at that very moment, she was glad that there was some opposition.

Luckily, his afternoon classes that day were easy ones. World geography and music appreciation. It was a good thing, too, because he had a hard enough time concentrating on what was taking place. His mind kept drifting back to the speech. He couldn't remember the faces so much as he did the sense of everyone listening. He could almost feel their ears curving, like old phonograph horns, in his direction. It was exciting and frightening at the same time.

". . . and one of the principal exports of Brazil is, let's see, hmmmm. Martinson?" a voice broke through.

"Coffee. Coffee beans, that is," he answered quickly. Whew, good thing the old reflexes are working, he thought.

"Well, I thought you might need a cup of coffee to wake you up, young man, but it seems you're still with us after all," Mr. Lawson intoned in his monotonous voice. "Now, let us continue."

Martin managed to keep alert for the remainder of the period, but he was glad when it was time to gather up his books and move on. In the corridors, on the way to the music room, he deliberately sought out classmates he didn't know well to see what their reactions might be — if there were any at all.

There were. Lots. Some clapped him on the back. A few looked at him from the corners of their eyes. One stared straight at him and drew an invisible circle 'round and 'round one ear, suggesting that Martin was crazy. A few silly girls just giggled when they saw him.

As he reached the door to the music room, he saw Howie. He couldn't hold in his curiosity for another second.

"What's up, Howie? What do you think?" he asked.

"I think Army's got it all over Navy, that's what."

"What are you talking about . . . oh, for cryin' out loud, Howie. Forget football for a minute. I'm talking about the speech. What have you heard?"

"Oh, everyone was talking about it in my English class, before old whatzisface came in. Everybody's heard about it if they weren't there. They noticed you, buddy, they noticed you."

"Geez," said Martin, "that's terrific, Howie. Thanks a lot. Hey, I'll see you later, we're going to be late. And I'll make you a gentleman's bet. I'll take Navy."

Within a few minutes he was in the music room, lost again in his memory of the first sweet taste of political combat as the voices around him sang out:

"There's a bower of roses by Bendemeer's stream . . ."

Interrupting his reverie, Martin laughed to himself. If Howie were here I'd tell him Bendemeer was a second-string placekicker for Notre Dame in the twenties. And I bet he'd believe me. All it takes is a little conviction.

At the end of the day, Martin was still keyed up over the reaction to the speech. He met Lester as he was shutting his locker and putting on his jacket.

"Listen, Les, I don't think I'm going to go home right away. I don't feel like settling down to my homework and the stuff I have to do at home. So I'm going to stop by my father's store and see if he wants me to do some work there. He can call my mother and tell her I'll be late. Wanna come with me?"

"Naw, I've gotta practice my clarinet. Yech! My mother's really after me for that 'cause I haven't put in two hours all week. Anyhow, I don't think your father likes me around."

"That's not true. He just didn't want you poking a pencil at the lobsters. Just 'cause they're lying there doesn't mean they're dead, you know. Hey, look, why don't you come over right away after you eat, before anyone else gets there? My mom loves it when you come over and have a second dessert with us. You practically licked the plate last time."

"Yeah, well, okay. What do you think you're having?"

"Probably guts pudding!" Martin leered.

"Yech, that's really awful. You're probably gonna be the first disgusting class president in the history of Taft."

"Yup," Martin continued. "And the cafeteria is going to serve Ground Walrus Tusk and *real* Frog Stew. And you know what, Lester, you're going to be the Chief Taster."

Lester smiled and thumbed his nose at Martin, and they set off in their separate directions.

Chapter 10

It usually took him about fifteen minutes to get from the school to his father's store. But today, since he wasn't expected, Martin took his time. He stopped now and then to talk and listen to one or two classmates who were walking in the same direction. Each time there was the same general conversation.

"Hey, that was some speech," they would say.

"Thanks," he would reply, "I hope you remember when it's time to vote."

"Sure thing," or something like that, they would answer, and the conversation would fade away.

Left alone, one part of Martin's mind would point out, Well, they didn't say that they would vote for you, did they?

Then the other part of his brain would counter with, No, but they didn't say they wouldn't, did they?

Then the first part would come back with, Well, a promise is a weak thing to begin with. So how good is what you just heard, anyhow?

Then the second voice would fight back with, Isn't it better than where you were before that speech? Huh?

And then, just as the first troublemaker inside his head was about to launch a new attack, Martin was face to face with the door of 152 Shirley Street and the "Martinson's" sign above it.

"Hi, Dad," he announced as he came in and set the bell jangling.

"Well, look who's here," said Mr. Martinson. "This must be my day for surprise visitors. Come on out and say hello, you rascal," he called over his shoulder to the back room where the walk-in refrigerator took up most of the space.

The big refrigerator door crunched shut and Martin heard the handle lock, to keep it airtight. With an armful of silvery mackerel nestled on a newspaper in his apron, Old Frank walked out. He deposited them on the working counter next to the sink.

"So, it's the politician come to pay us a campaign call, is it?" he asked at the sight of Martin. "Now, are you looking for a little contribution for campaign expenses? Or maybe you just want me to come down to that school and tell those kids who the best man for the job is. What do you say there, sonny?"

Martin grinned at him. "No, it's not that. I'm doing okay, so far, I guess, Old Frank. I just didn't feel like going right home so I thought I'd stop by and see if there was anything I could do to help out. But it looks like you beat me to it."

"Oh, there were one or two things I didn't get done on Friday, so I came in to get your old man to buy me a free cup of coffee while I finished up. We might get him to spring for a glass of milk and a doughnut for you, too, if you'll go across the street and get it for us. How does that sound?"

"Great," said Martin and in a few seconds he was on his way. Soon he was back with the cardboard cups of coffee for his father and Old Frank and the milk and doughnut for himself.

"Doesn't look like we're going to be interrupted by customers, does it?" said Mr. Martinson.

"Oh, come on, you know Mondays are always slow at a fish market," said Old Frank. "Besides, this gives us a chance to get a real campaign report from the candidate himself. How are things going, Martin?"

Martin licked the doughnut crumbs off his lower lip and told them what had taken place at the lunchtime rally. He even included the part where the cry of "Marty-Smarty" had started up.

"Do you think that will give you much trouble?" asked his father. "Or is it still 'sticks and stones' as far as you're concerned?"

"I really don't know. I can't figure it out yet," Martin answered. "I guess it all depends on *how* they say it, you know, if it sounds like they're calling me a name, a bad one. What a dumb nickname, anyhow!"

"Now don't go knocking nicknames. Look at mine. It doesn't bother me," said Old Frank.

90

"Why should it?" said Martin quickly. "After all . . . oops!"

Both Mr. Martinson and Old Frank burst into laughter.

"Boy, I sure put my foot in my mouth that time," apologized Martin.

"Coming from someone else, I might mind. But I know you didn't have mean thoughts when you said it. And it's true," said Old Frank. "I deserve it now. But I've been called that for more years than I can tell you. Since I was just a tad, even younger than you."

Martin didn't dare look at his father for fear that he would burst into giggles. They had both heard this story many times before, but Old Frank loved to tell it and he didn't really mind listening.

"You see," Old Frank went on, "I used to go out to the fish piers way back then. My father was in the business, too, just like your granddad in the whole-sale market. And I was such a little fella, nobody hardly noticed me. I was kind of shy, too, just hangin' around in the background while the grown-ups went about their business.

"Well, one day, a bunch of them got to arguing about something to do with that day's catch and the price of the fish. Going at it pretty strong, too. And one would claim, 'Don't tell me! Old Bill here knows a thing or two.' And another would say, 'Now you just can't put one over on old Fred here.' And then somebody else would pipe in, 'You just leave every-thing to old Tom.'

"I can't tell you how long this went on, but I'd already had my breakfast as well as the hardboiled egg my mother had given me to take along, and probably an apple, and I don't know what else. I just wolfed it down back then.

"Anyhow, all that good food had gotten working away in my insides and I started feeling funny. I tried to tell them, they were so busy with themselves, they just paid me no attention. Until it hit me all of a sudden. I started to run away, but it was too late. I upchucked right behind a barrel of cod. And then, one of them said, 'Hey, what's that funny smell?' Then they looked around and finally noticed me. Somebody grabbed hold of me and took me to my father, who was right in the middle of it all, and he asked, 'What's the matter, boy?' And I just had to tell him, so I bawled out in front of everyone, 'Old Frank just threw up!' Well, they took to howling and that made such an impression you can imagine how the story spread. The name just stuck and I've been called 'Old Frank' ever since."

"See, Martin," said his father after he stopped laughing. "Be grateful you didn't end up with a worse nickname. Oh, boy, that's some story. Listen, I don't mind you being here, son, but there's nothing you can really do around this place today. So, why don't you head on home and give your mother a help-ing hand if she needs it. And as for you, old-timer, you get any funny feelings, you just drop everything and head downstairs to the little room with the white porcelain fixtures."

He was about to send Martin off with a pat when he gave a little groan.

"Oh-oh," he said, "here come the Anderson ladies to spend an hour deciding between the halibut and the haddock. If you don't want to get caught up in that one, the two of you had better get on with it. So long, son. . . . Ah, good afternoon, ladies. And, what can we do for you today?"

"I was interested in, let's see . . . hmmmm . . . the halibut," said one Miss Anderson.

"The haddock looks a little fresher," said the other.

Chapter 11

"I'll get it," yelled Helena as she dashed out of her room and raced for the telephone.

"Slow down, young lady, slow down. You don't have to go and break a leg just 'cause *he* talked to you today," called her mother from the kitchen.

"Oh, Mother," sighed Helena. "Hello? Oh, Nancy, I'm so glad it's you. . . ." and her voice trailed off as she stretched the telephone cord so that it just reached into her bedroom. She shut the door and, once she was safe beyond hearing, she went on, "What do you mean, 'What do I think?' I think he's genuinely interested, that's what."

A long pause while she listened to the voice at the other end of the line.

"Look, Nancy, someone doesn't spend all that much time talking to someone else when someone might easily have said just a few words and let it go at that. Unless that first someone was interested in some small way, shape, or form in that someone else.

That's all I'm saying. I'm not trying to turn it into a big thing, you know."

Another pause. A shorter one.

"Okay, Nance, I understand what you're saying and I'm perfectly willing to look at it from another, what did you say? Oh, right, *objective* point of view. But I'm not willing to dismiss the possibility — mind you, I'm just saying 'the possibility' — that there might be something more to this, something that could lead to something."

The briefest pause of all. Then . . .

"Uh huh. Uh huh. Uh huh. Uh huh. Right, Nancy, right . . . sure. Well, look, I gotta go now. My mother wants me to help her fix the salad for supper. What do you mean? I can wash lettuce, can't I? Look, I'll see you tomorrow. No, I'm going to do my homework here tonight. Yeah, I'll see you. 'Bye."

Helena replaced the receiver firmly; you couldn't exactly call it slamming the phone down. She had barely gotten up from her cross-legged position on the floor near the door when the phone rang again.

"I have it," she called back to her mother. "Hello? Inez, I don't believe it. I just hung up on Nancy this very minute."

In soft tones, the entire previous conversation was retold as best Helena could remember. Nancy's opinion was voted on, dismissed, and the two began again to review the significance of the encounter with Rick Petersen on the steps at lunchtime.

"I'm certainly glad that I have one friend who can

be a little *objective* about things and see them in their true light," Helena sighed into the telephone. "Listen, I'd love to ask you over here to do homework with me tonight, but Martin is having Lester and some of his gang in for a political meeting. Couldn't you die? Anyhow, it would be too crowded. So why don't I come over there? What? You got the new Dick Haymes record? Fabulous! Look, I'll be over as soon as we're through after supper. Okay? 'Bye . . . oh, Inez, I just want to tell you, you really are a true friend."

"Boy, look at this place. A piece of dirt wouldn't be caught dead here!" Stevie let out a low whistle.

Martin's room was immaculate. Not only was the bed neatly made, but all the usual clutter had been removed, stacked away on closet shelves or tucked into drawers. Two of the kitchen chairs plus his own maple armchair, his desk chair, and the backless seat from under his mother's sewing machine were arranged in a circle. And on each chair there was a pad of paper and a freshly sharpened pencil.

"Okay, if everybody will take a seat, and we have to use the bed, too, we can get started," announced Lester, who had put his pad of paper into a clipboard.

"All right, I'm on the bed, so where's my paper?" asked Howie.

"Here, take this off that chair. I'll use that one," said Lester.

"Looks like this is going to be all business," murmured Bobby. "I don't see nothin' to read. Hey, Martin, where's the comic books and magazines 'n everything?"

"We'll get to the good stuff as soon as we finish up with the campaign, Bobby," Martin replied. "Don't worry, it won't take long. In fact, let's skip the 'Calling the Meeting to Order' and get right down to business. Okay?"

They shouted their agreement.

"All right," he went on, "let's have a report on how you all figure it went today. Lester, why don't you start off."

Lester stood up. "I think the speech today was great and all afternoon I heard kids talking all about it and asking whose idea it was. . . ."

"Betcha told it was yours," came from Bernie.

"Nope, I said it was the candidate's own idea and that we just helped him with it. Scout's honor."

"Hah! Scout's honor!" shouted Howie, "You're not even a scout."

"C'mon, guys," Martin urged.

Stevie got off the bed and stood in the middle. "Look, we've all talked about it, and everybody agrees it was terrific. The whole class knows you're really in there and you're going to fight. And that's what counts, isn't it?"

"Sure," said Martin, "but did anyone mention what I talked about?"

"Well," Howie offered, "I heard some guys saying that it was a lot of talk, but what can you do about it?

97

I mean, who's gonna make the school change and give us good seats at the games? That's what I heard."

"Hey, someone actually got what I said. Oh, boy, wait till we tell them the plan. All the stuff we wrote down last meeting — pickets, boycotts, a strike, all that," said Martin.

"Do you really think that'll work?" asked Lester.

"C'mon, Les, you forgot what I told you last time. It doesn't really matter whether or not your ideas work. A candidate's gotta have lots of ideas. That's what counts."

"Yeah," said Bobby. "And Normie Sands hasn't had three ideas in the last ten years. In fact, the only idea anybody ever heard him come up with is 'Hey, let's have a party!'"

"Sure, but that's a pretty good idea," answered Bernie.

Martin persisted, "It's more important to come up with stuff that's good for everyone, not just the privileged kids who get invited to his parties."

"Don't forget," said Stevie, "everyone still kind of likes him. He doesn't have any real enemies."

And so the discussion went, back and forth, for the next half hour. Eventually everyone had his say, every opinion was voiced, and agreement about new plans was reached by exhaustion, if not total assent.

"So," Lester stood in the middle of the group and summed up, "tomorrow we go through with Part Two. We get out the milk crates and Martin makes a speech telling about the pickets and the strike if the

98

school won't give us better seats. And this time, he makes sure to tell them that this is just one of his ideas and that a vote for him means some brains working for the class, not just a lot of back-slapping. Okay? Finally? Huh?"

"All right, all right. So what do we have all this paper 'n stuff for, anyhow?" asked Howie.

"That was Lester's idea," said Martin. "In case anybody here got any brainstorms."

There was a knock on the door. Mrs. Martinson entered with her biggest mixing bowl covered with a napkin cradled in her arms.

"Can I interest any of the hard-working politicians in this room in some fresh popcorn?"

"Oh, boy, great."

"Hey, thank you, thanks a lot."

"Let's hear it for the president's mother," shouted Stevie.

A round of applause and scattered shouts of agreement were sounded as she left the room.

"Now, I have a surprise, too," said Martin. "Stevie, if you'll get off the bed and lift that bedspread, you can take out that box underneath. Here," and he dragged the box over to where he was sitting.

"Because you've been a lot of help, I want to show my appreciation. These are all my comic books for the last year, the ones I was saving to swap next time we had a trading session. Instead, I'm gonna give them to you. Here, you can have them all; take what you want."

99

"Wow! Look, here's a practically new *House of Horror!*"

"Hey, I never even saw this one before. It's about you, Lester. *Les Miserables*," said Howie, making it sound like "less mizrubbles."

"Aw, that's one of Martin's old Classic Comics. It's originally in French. Now that we're studying it in school, no wonder you're dumping that," answered Lester.

"Have some more popcorn, Lester," Martin offered, pushing the bowl in his direction. There was no reason to tell them that he hadn't much looked at comic books for about a year now. Somehow or other, this wasn't the time to talk about that. Or anything like his new interest in Shakespeare. It just didn't seem to mix very well with politics.

Chapter 12

M r. Lindstrom finished arranging everything on the tray to his satisfaction. The crisp triangles of toast were spread with butter that had softened during the morning. In the center of the plate were thinly sliced stacks of lean roast beef and cubes of tangy Swiss cheese. A small paper cup contained tiny vinegary pickles. His neatly folded napkin was tucked under one edge of the plate, near the wooden pepper mill and salt shaker. Shiny silver was laid out in its proper place, too. And, at the top right-hand corner were a white porcelain cup and saucer with fresh black coffee that had just been delivered from the cafeteria.

No, he thought to himself, I don't like those mugs everyone's using. They're just uncivilized.

Carrying the tray across the room to the little two-seat couch, he lowered it to a small table upon which rested an unopened copy of the morning *Herald*.

He sat down with a sigh of pleasure and began to

nibble at the toast and read the front page of "a sensible paper which gives you the facts," when he became aware of more noise outside that he was accustomed to hearing at this hour.

He tried to ignore it, to go on with his reading and his lunch, but it was growing undeniably louder. And louder. And *much louder*.

"This is ridiculous," he muttered to himself. "Leave this place for one day to go to a conference and heaven only knows what goes on around here." He got up out of the soft, cushiony seat and went over to the window.

Within seconds his eyes grew wider and wider until they appeared to be larger than the lenses of the glasses that were almost sliding off his nose as his jaw dropped.

On this bright and sunny fall day, there were more students outside than he had ever noticed before. But instead of just meandering about as they usually did, circling casually around like goldfish in a bowl, they were gathered in small clusters. There were several little crowds, each surrounding a central figure who was standing on something and shouting and waving his or her fists.

They were everywhere. In the forecourt, on the front steps. Atop the short brick columns that formed the decorative entry to the schoolyard. Milk-carton platforms had been erected in front of the trees. Small mobs of listeners surrounded shouting orators.

And, good grief, what was that white and shiny monstrosity parked right next to the playing-field bleachers? An ice cream wagon? For goodness sakes! Students were lined up for almost fifty yards, just waiting to gorge themselves on treats strictly forbidden to be sold on school property.

It was chaos. It was madness. It was not allowed.

"Miss Bellini!" he called, without realizing that he was shouting directly at the glass and not in her direction.

"Miss Bellini!" he repeated. Then, realizing he was getting no response, he turned and stormed into the outer office.

Miss Bellini and her two assistants were unaware of his entrance. They were crowded up against the windows, laughing, pointing, picking out figures, and commenting on the commotion outside.

"Ahem!" Mr. Lindstrom cleared his throat. "Ahem!" No one paid attention. Finally, he said, "Well, ladies," in a booming voice, "I seem to have interrupted the spectators in the gallery. Would one of you mind telling me, what on earth is that Roman circus going on outside this school? Has the student body gone mad? Or am I hallucinating?"

"Oh, Mr. Lindstrom," giggled Miss Bellini, "I didn't see you come in." She nudged the others to get busy and quickly sat down at her desk.

"Well, my question is still unanswered. What, pray tell, is this nonsense all about out there and who gave

103

them permission to do whatever they're doing, anyhow?"

"I'm sorry, sir," she finally replied. "I don't think anyone gave them permission. I don't think they even thought of asking. You see, it's the election coming up, and I guess they're all out there campaigning."

"Campaigning? Whatever gave them the idea to do that? We've never had this kind of . . . er . . . *tumultuous involvement* before. Don't they realize that all this noise, this commotion is something we've never had at this school. It's just, just . . . just *not done.*"

Running up and down stairs. Slamming doors. Forgetting to say "Sir" or Ma'am" to a teacher. Shouting. Entering without knocking. Laughing too loud. All these were "not done." Mr. Lindstrom's mental list went on and on, without ever being published officially. And, up until now, it had included vigorous political campaigning. Rather, the school set aside one assembly day, just before the balloting took place, when the candidates were given an opportunity to address their classmates. Then, during the closing homeroom period the ballot boxes were brought around and the votes were cast. After school, a faculty committee counted them, and the next morning the results were posted on the bulletin boards. It was all very civilized. The way it should be. Anything else was simply "not done."

"How did they ever get this nonsense into their

heads? Don't tell me that it was a case of spontaneous inspiration among them all. I can't believe that."

Miss Bellini ran her fingers lightly along the keys of her typewriter and cast her eyes down.

"It . . . uh . . . actually started yesterday. Uh, that is, well, in a small way. You see, we didn't think there was anything wrong. It was actually sort of . . . amusing. I mean, we thought it was."

"Could you please tell me exactly what took place in my absence yesterday?" he asked.

She related the story of Martin's surprising arrival on the scene and how they had just caught the tail end of his speech on the milk crates. As she had observed it from the window, he had just been asking for votes and it didn't appear to be causing a serious disturbance. In fact, everyone in the office had admired his initiative.

"Martinson, hm? Not enough work for him to do in his classes, I suppose. Strange, I never pictured him as a troublemaker," said Mr. Lindstrom.

"Do you really think that this will cause trouble?" Miss Bellini ventured to ask.

"Well, it looks harmless enough on the outside. But that's how it starts. Next thing you know they'll be parading up and down with signs, asking for extra holidays and no homework and all sorts of nonsense. You have to be on the lookout. You can't take any chance on letting the lunatics run the asylum. Oh, dear, what I am I saying? That's not what I mean. I'd better look into this. Don't you all have any work to do?" he shouted as he turned back into his office and, for the first time any of the secretaries could remember, he slammed the door.

For a few minutes, they didn't even dare look at each other or whisper a word. Finally, when they realized that the noise outside prevented him from hearing their conversation, they started buzzing at one another again.

Under her breath, with a sly smile toward the window and the commotion outside, Miss Bellini mumbled, "Good luck, Martinson, good luck. You're going to need it."

Unaware that they were being observed by such a startled spectator, the schoolyard politicians shouted away. Martin and Lester stood off to one side of the proceedings, their gaze sweeping in the whole scene. Periodic reports came back to them by a series of runners — Bobby, Billy, Howie, and Stevie.

"I don't believe it," panted Stevie, out of breath from the long trek back from a far corner. "Nancy Hodges is promising to lower the dues if she's elected treasurer. She says we only end up giving the money to the school to buy library books, anyhow. And everyone's just eating it up."

"Talk about eating it up," announced Howie as he arrived on the scene, "do you believe what Normie did? Look at that line at the ice cream truck. He's calling it a 'pre-victory preview' and he's giving away ice cream to the whole class if they want it."

"That's 'cause he wouldn't know what to say if he had to get up and talk to anyone," scowled Lester.

"You know what they say," answered Howie. "Action talks better'n words. Those who's got it spend it."

Yeah, thought Martin, and those who know they're gonna get it . . . right on the chin . . . sometimes run in the house. But he didn't mention his run-in with Normie on Walnut Place. He'd heard enough fish stories to know that no one was interested in the one that got away.

"I guess his father didn't have enough time to get someone to write a speech for him overnight. So this is the next best thing," said Stevie.

Bobby straggled over to the group and held up two popsicles.

"Hey, anybody want one of these? They ran out of Fudgsicles, so I got two of these instead," he announced.

"Naw," answered Lester, "I couldn't eat 'enemy ice cream.'"

"Go ahead, Les," said Martin. "Maybe it'll help you stay cool. Come to think of it, I'll have half of the grape, Bobby. Here comes Bernie. Give him the rest."

"Boy," said Bernie as he reached for the purple treat, "just listen to them. I guess just about everyone who's running for office in every class is out here drumming up . . . what? Business?"

"You know, guys, how we talked last night about how we figured everyone was going to climb on our bandwagon? Well, it looks like they stole it instead," said Martin.

"Sure," Lester agreed, "you come up with a good idea, a way to kind of shake people up, and look what happens. Now everybody wants to get into the act."

"Everybody wants to have his own act," said Bobby, licking his fingers. "But nobody's original. Geez, Martin, whatcha want to be president of this pack for, anyhow?"

"Aw, c'mon, Bobby, lay off," said Howie.

"I don't know, Bobby," sighed Martin. "It seemed like a good idea when I thought about it." He paused. "And it's still a good idea. I really think I could do some things for the class, so we could all have a better time going to Taft while we're here. Hey, guys, come on. This isn't the end of it. We're not finished yet."

"You don't think so?" said Marilyn Tracey as she walked by them, licking a coconut-covered vanilla ice cream cone like a plump, contented cat. "How are you going to get anyone's attention now, Mr. Marty-Smarty?" And with that, she turned into the crowd.

"Fickle, very fickle," snapped Stevie.

"But she's right about one thing," said Martin. "We really have to work to get the kids to listen to us now. Oh, boy. We'd better start thinking about some new strategy. Let's talk about it after supper tonight."

"Gee, Martin," said Lester, "I don't know if my mother will let me out two nights in a row. She's really after me to do my homework."

"Me, too," said Bobby.

108

"That goes for me," said Bernie.

Before anyone else could join in, Martin said, "OK, let's not have a meeting tonight. We'll take a night off. But, if anyone thinks of anything, let's talk on the phone, okay?"

"Agreed," came the reply.

They headed into the school, each trying to think of something better than free ice cream. There had to be something. But what?

Mrs. McManus slashed the words across the blackboard: "Pages 112 through 114, Problems 1–10, 14–18 and 22–28."

"I expect you to have these completed for class tomorrow," she announced. "There will be a quiz at the end of the week, and we must cover this area if we are to get on with things. Don't even bother showing up for class if you have not completed the assignment."

Groans and mutters continued right through the ringing of the bell as the class arose to leave.

"Honest," said Sally Wilson, a quiet, very intelligent girl who sat right next to Martin, "I think she's going crazy. That's more than she's ever given us before. I wonder what's gotten into her."

"No fooling, Sally," said Rick Petersen. He had joined up with her and Martin as they headed off for their next, and last, class. "I don't know how I'm going to get it done. You live so close to my house, could I stop over? Can you give me a hand tonight?"

"I'd love to," she replied, "but we're going over to my grandmother's for her birthday dinner, so I'm going to have to work on it right after school, while you're in practice."

"Darn," he grumbled. "Well, Martinson, old man, it looks as though I may just have to take up your sister's offer."

"Helena? Are you kidding? She's in the other class and they're 'way behind us," Martin answered. He was still thinking about the lunchtime scenes in the schoolyard and had hardly paid attention until Rick had mentioned his sister. Using that catchword, he was able to retrace the half-heard conversation and reply as though he had been listening carefully all the time.

"Right," laughed Rick. "But she didn't offer to help me herself. She offered *you*."

"You're kidding. It's like slavery. She thinks she owns me. Aw, I don't mind, though. Sure, come on over tonight if you want and we'll work it out."

"Aren't you going to have to work on your political campaign?" asked Sally as they arrived at the stairway where they had to split up. "I saw what happened outside today. Looks like your rival has increased his popularity."

"Yeah, well, my friends and I have some ideas, but we're going to take a night off to work things out on our own. So I guess I can spare some time for Rick. Boy, that's all I have to do, just let word out that I wouldn't help the captain of the football team with his math. Boy! Would that ever mess things up!"

"Hey, wait a minute," said Rick. "It won't be all that tough. I'm not exactly dumb myself, you know. I *did* get elected captain, didn't I? Maybe I can swap some political pointers for help in math."

"It's a deal," nodded Martin. "See you tonight."

Late that afternoon, Mrs. Martinson decided to reward herself for finishing her shopping in record time. She dropped off her bundles at the fish market and walked across the street to the bakery, where she could sit and have a cup of coffee at one of their little tables.

"Hi, Gloria," she said to one of the women behind the busy counter as she sat down at one side of the shop. "I'll have coffee and a bran muffin whenever you have a chance."

"Let me get you a fresh one. They're still warm. Here," Gloria said as she arrived at the table a few minutes later with the steaming cup and the muffin.

As she turned toward the counter, she nearly collided with a tall, very well-dressed woman walking by.

"Oh, excuse me, I didn't see you, Mrs. Sands," she apologized.

"That's all right, dear," Mrs. Sands replied. "No harm done. Just be careful, now."

Suddenly, Mrs. Martinson spoke out, "And excuse me, but are you Norman Sands' mother?"

"Why, yes, I am." Mrs. Sands frowned, her brow forming the unspoken question: Why do you ask?

"I should explain," Mrs. Martinson went on. "I'm Barbara Martinson, Martin's mother. It seems that our sons are running against each other in the school election and I thought I should say 'hello.' I suppose it seems silly now, but it just struck me as Gloria mentioned your name."

Mrs. Sands relaxed her compressed look. She said, "Oh, I'm glad you did. It's nice to meet you. I'd love to stay and get acquainted, but I must pick up an order. We're expecting quite a crowd of Norman's friends over this evening. Ah, politics! It certainly keeps the young ones busy. And us, too. Isn't this a wonderful shop? I buy all our pastry here. I'll probably have them make the victory cake, too. Well, I must run. It certainly has been a pleasure."

The door had barely shut before Mrs. Martinson blurted out, "Well, I like that! Victory cake, indeed! She's pretty cocky. Hmmmm. We'll just see."

Gloria leaned over the counter. "Did someone open a refrigerator door? Or was that an iceberg that just sailed through?"

"Iceberg? Hah! More like an ice cube. Gloria, here, let me pay you. I've got to get going. There's work to be done on this election and there's no time to lose."

"Yeah, hello? Oh, hi, Normie." Stevie spoke into the telephone. "No, I didn't know it was you, no. Right, I was surprised. Huh? Huh? Oh, gee, thanks,

112

but I don't think I could come over. No, I've got a lot of homework to do — 'n things. No, I am not going over to Martin's house. I'm going nowhere except to do my English.

"Look, Normie, I don't have nothing against you. I never said I did. Hey, Martin's a friend of mine and . . . what? Well, is that a fact? Well, Normie, don't be surprised if you just get a different picture after you've talked to enough other kids.

"Hey, Normie . . . what? Sure, I like to have fun. Sure, I like to go to parties. Hey, but there's some things more important, you know. Like friendship.

"Look, maybe someday we'll be really good friends. But I'll tell you something. Right now I gotta give my vote to Martin. And I gotta help him get elected.

"Normie, hey, don't be such a sore sport. You know something? You're gonna make a really poor loser.

"G'bye."

Chapter 13

Dinnertime at the Martinson household was particularly quiet that evening. Mr. Martinson had arrived early with a little treat, shrimp that he had shelled, ready for the pot. Mrs. Martinson had quickly cooked them. Then they were chilled and heaped on shredded lettuce around a small bowl of hot, spicy cocktail sauce, with just a little horseradish for zest.

But Martin listlessly picked at his shrimp and Helena chewed silently on hers. Mrs. Martin talked quietly to her husband about the usual household matters. Not much interest was shown about anything until she mentioned bumping into Mrs. Sands.

You could practically see Martin's ears perk up as he asked, "Did she have anything to say? What was she doing? Does she think Normie's going to win? Did she say anything about the election?"

The questions flew out, one after another. The shrimp were forgotten, a warm biscuit on his plate lay unbuttered, and he almost put his fork into his water glass as he tried to appear casual and waited for an answer.

Carefully presenting the story to make it sound as inoffensive as possible, Mrs. Martinson told them most of what had happened. She wisely left out her own violent reaction and even suggested that she had laughed off the encounter.

"So you see," she concluded, "she's just another mother who's trying to be helpful to her children. Now, dear," to Martin, "remember, all you have to do is ask us if you want any help. I'm not suggesting that you *buy* your votes with cookies — which I would gladly bake — but, if there's anything, well, you know where to turn."

Martin got up from his place and went over to her and gave her a strong hug around the shoulders and laid his face next to hers, something he had not done for a long time.

"Thank you," he whispered in a husky voice and went back to his seat.

"Well, I could certainly use some help," announced Helena. "I have to finish my homework, do the dishes, fold my laundry . . ."

"Make a few phone calls," interjected Mr. Martinson.

"Right, I have to talk to Inez. And then I have to iron a blouse for tomorrow . . ." she went on.

"I guess, then, you'll probably be too busy to say hello when Rick stops by," Martin mentioned very casually.

115

"Rick? Rick who? You don't mean . . . *Rick Petersen?*" the astonished Helena managed to blurt out.

"Yep," said Martin. "Comin' over to do a little math with his pal Martin. Seems like some wicked witch laid a curse on her kid brother and offered him up as a sacrifice."

"Martin, no name-calling. You take that back," ordered his mother.

"OK, I take it back. But anyhow, Rick's coming over after supper 'cause we had a huge homework assignment in math and he needs some help. So you better go stick some pins in your hair, Helena. He'll be here pretty soon."

That evening one member of the family whipped through dinner and her chores in record speed. She had retired to her bedroom behind a firmly closed door when the doorbell rang.

Curiosity drove Mrs. Martinson to answer it before anyone else could make a move. After all, who was this Galahad who had captured her daughter's . . . well, maybe not her heart, but certainly her attention.

The young man at the door was good-looking and, right away, he seemed likable enough.

"You must be Rick Petersen. Martin told us you'd be over to work on your math. Why don't you come on in and I'll let Martin show you to his dungeon."

"Hi, Rick, come on back here," called Martin, and in a few minutes they were huddled under the desk light, scratching out numbers all over sheets and sheets of blank arithmetic paper.

They had kept the door shut to keep from being disturbed during the torturous session, so they hadn't seen Helena emerge from her room and position herself strategically opposite the doorway to the living room. But when they finished and came out to see about a glass of milk as a reward for their labors, Rick caught sight of her immediately.

"Oh, hi," she said casually, curled up in the big overstuffed chair, almost as though she barely knew who he was.

"Hi, yourself," he replied warmly. "Hey, I really have to thank you for setting me up with Martin. He's not only good in math, he's a great teacher. We really whipped through that assignment. Oh, I'm sorry, sir, I'm Rick Petersen. You must be Mr. Martinson."

"Yes, I'm the father of this pair," replied Mr. Martinson, getting up from the sofa and heading for the kitchen. "I'd better see if I can give my wife a hand. I think she's putting together a little something for us all."

A little while later they were all sitting around the living room, drinking hot chocolate and nibbling on crumbly lemon squares. Mr. Martinson had talked enthusiastically to Rick about football and Taft's problems with its running game. Helena, who was satisfied at the attention she had gotten from Rick during the few minutes they were alone, helped her

117

mother unravel a mess of yarn in her knitting bag. And Martin sat quietly taking it all in.

His mind drifted in and out of the conversation, which flowed smoothly on and made few demands on him. Most of the time he was miles away.

The warm feeling of contentment in the room held him for a few minutes, but it was soon displaced by thoughts of the election. He began to wonder about why he was running for office. Did he really want to be president? Could he really do the job? Would he be more popular if he were elected or would it cause new problems?

One by one he answered the questions, silently. And one by one new questions appeared. It was like swimming against the tide; he was doing a lot of work and getting nowhere.

"What do you say, Drifter?" he heard his father say.

Before he could acknowledge that he had lost track of what they'd been talking about, Rick asked, "What did you call him? Drifter?"

Mr. Martinson explained, "That's right, Drifter. When he was just a little nipper, he had a habit of slowly fading off while you were having a conversation. His eyes would glaze over . . . just so. Mind you, he wouldn't fall asleep, just sort of drift in and out. So, Barbara and I started calling him Drifter. But, Lord, we haven't used that in a long time."

Martin spoke up, "Go ahead, have your fun. Pick

on a guy while he's down. May I have another one of those squares, please?"

"You really are involved in this election, aren't you?" Rick asked. "Boy, you sure turned the school around with that soapbox speech the other day. Looked like the time I was in Boston on a Sunday morning and we went by the Common. Just like that, all those guys perched out there preaching and shouting."

A smile crept across Martin's face and he said, quietly, "I know; that's where I got the idea."

Helena cut in, "But look what happened. Now everybody's doing it and nobody really listens to anyone anymore. It's a big circus. Nobody is serious about elections at Taft. They never were, and they probably never will be."

"I know in the three years I've been there," said Rick, "I've never seen so much made of an election. I wonder what the school — you know, Lindstrom and the teachers — think about it. I haven't heard anything."

"My best friend, Inez McMullen, said that her U.S. history teacher said that it was the best thing that happened at Taft since they started collecting for the Red Feather," said Helena. "It gives everyone a chance to really get involved in democracy and not just take it for granted."

"But Bobby and Lester told me that in their English class, Mr. Wozniak said that it was a whole lot of nonsense, a bunch of kids making a lot of noise and not even knowing what they were shouting about," Martin said, wiping the lemon-flavored crumbs off his chin and licking his fingers.

"Use a napkin, young man," ordered Mrs. Martinson.

"Well, I think it's terrific," said Rick. "I agree with Martin that the seventh-graders are treated badly about football tickets . . . and a whole lot of other things. And they — heck, *we* — all should have a chance to do something about it. I don't know if it'll do you any good, fella, but I'm behind you. All the way."

"Martin, isn't it time you let us in on what you're going to do?" asked his mother. "You have those closed-door meetings with Lester and Howie and the others and you all come out with your lips buttoned up. Look, your father and I can make signs as well as the next person. And here's Rick, able-bodied and willing. And Helena. Well, she'll help, too. Now just tell us what you want us to do."

"Uh, well, I'm not sure if there's anything anyone else can do right now. I . . . uh . . . I've got some work and, well, I'm not ready for any help. Right now, that is," he said.

Everyone could tell he had something in mind, some plan he wasn't ready to reveal quite yet.

Mr. Martinson gave his wife one of those looks that said, Leave it alone for now. Don't push him.

"Enough of this talk about politics," she announced.

"It's still early, so I say, how about a game of Parcheesi?"

"I'd love it," said Rick.

Helena groaned but went to fetch the board.

Chapter 14

Martin did have a plan. He had always kept the idea in the back of his mind. Every time it inched forward, he had shoved it back. But it kept returning and the time had finally come when he had to face it, look it squarely head on, and decide whether or not to use it.

There was a high risk involved, higher than anything he had ever attempted before. And he wasn't even sure he could carry it off. But the campaign was running out of steam. He had to try to keep it alive, to get it going once again.

The next morning, Lester arrived on time and they were able to start off for school without hurrying.

"So what do you think, Martin?" Lester asked, about thirty seconds into the trip.

"About what?"

"About the campaign, the election. What else?"

122

"Oh, yeah, gee, Les. I don't know right this minute what to do."

Lester looked at him quizzically. "Didn't you work on it last night? After we talked on the phone? Didn't you come up with some ideas?"

Martin replied, "To tell you what, I really didn't do a lot on it. We had a ton of math to do and I had to work on that. And besides that, Rick Petersen came over for some help."

"Rick Petersen? You're kidding."

"No, honest. Helena offered him my help in math 'cause he caught her when she tripped or something. So last night I paid off for her."

"Oh yeah, so is that all you did last night?"

"No, we played Parcheesi, too."

"Parcheesi! Boy, it sounds like you all had some party. I guess you don't care about the election anymore."

"Aw, c'mon, Les. The whole family was there and Rick and we talked a little bit about the election, and he told everyone what a big hit the speech was the other day. And how everyone else is doing it now."

Lester pressed on. "What else did he say? Did he give you any clues how he got elected captain of the football team?"

"As a matter of fact, he did mention it. He said that sometimes excellence is so obvious that it just has to be rewarded."

123

"Really?"

"No, I'm just pulling your leg. But he was OK. And he said he was behind me, for whatever that was worth."

"Hah! A lotta good . . ."

Martin cut in, "Take it easy, Lester. I know Rick's help doesn't mean much, but it's better than having him — or anyone in the whole school — against me. 'Sides, we've got a little time and we don't have to go nuts rushing into things that won't work out."

"You're right, Mart," answered Lester. "We have to plan the next move very carefully, so's no one can copy it like the last one. What say we have a meeting tonight at my house? I don't think my mother will mind."

Martin hesitated. "Uh, I'm not sure. I, uh, don't know how much homework I'll have. Uh, math 'n everything, you know. Why don't we talk about it after school? Okay?"

"Golly, Martin, don't you, I mean, can't you . . . I mean, gee, Martin, shouldn't you count on working on the election first and then figure out when to do your homework? Huh?"

"Lester, we're here to get an education," Martin said, slowly and firmly, but without a lot of conviction.

Chapter 15

The second period of the four morning sessions was over. For the seven minutes during which the students were allowed to go to their lockers to get new books or gym equipment, most of the faculty headed for the teacher's lounge on the second floor. It was a cosy, high-ceilinged room over which a cloud of cigarette smoke hovered during breaks.

"And how are the little monsters responding to their first encounters with the language of Victor Hugo and de Maupassant, John?" asked Mrs. Burns, the General Science teacher.

Mr. Martin drew slowly on his filtered cigarette and replied, "Like the Hun. They approach it like a stone wall to be beaten down and they massacre it with their pronunciation. 'Ler livruh est sur lar tarbull.' Grrr . . . !"

"Hah!" she laughed. "You ought to hear them referring to Archimedes as 'Archie' when they think I'm not listening. Oh, well, they'll get it eventually. And at least there's the consolation of the good ones, you know. At least some of them show some spark in their eyes and not the usual vacant stare when you ask a question."

"Yes," said Mrs. McManus, sitting in the corner of the room, knitting a gray scarf. "But even they disappoint you, too. Even the best of them. Even the best."

"Sounds like one of Martha's *favorites* has let her down," said Mr. Martin with a heavy accent on the last syllable, to give the word a foreign flavor.

"Not a favorite, no, no, not at all. Just a very promising young man who could easily lead the class. I always thought I could tell, but not the way he behaved this morning. Dumb! He acted just plain dumb!"

"Who is it?" asked Mrs. Burns. "You said a 'young man.' I thought you were going to tell me about Judy Rosen. I happen to think she's about the brightest youngster in this school. I'm glad it's not Judy."

"No, no," replied Mrs. McManus. "It's the Martinson boy. You know, the one they advanced to my ninth-grade class. His tests were so good there was no doubt that he was just coasting along in the seventh grade. He even glided through the eighth-grade material in the exams. And when he came into my class, he seemed to take to it. But today, oh my goodness, today you wouldn't have believed he knew the two table. Such a disappointment."

"Maybe it's this election. You know he's running for class president. You heard what happened outside after lunch the other day. Maybe that's what's gotten to him," offered Mr. Kelley, looking up from his newspaper.

"That's probably it," Mrs. McManus sputtered, jabbing the long needles at each other and into the gray wool. "That's just the trouble around here. Too much emphasis on extracurricular activities. Sports and clubs and all that. Too much. Much too much. Now . . ."

"Martha, don't get yourself all worked up." Mrs. Burns went over and patted her on the arm and then bent down to pick up the ball of yarn, which had fallen from her lap. "You know, when you think of it, what's so terrible about calling him 'Archie' as long as they remember what he did."

"What *did* he do?" asked Mr. Martin.

"He discovered the word *Eureka!*" roared Mr. Kelley, and they all laughed.

The seventh-graders were used to surprises. Birthday parties, hurricanes . . . all kinds.

But for pure shock, nothing could have astonished them more than Martin Martinson's performance in the spelling bee that morning.

"If I wasn't there myself, I never would have believed it," said Marilyn Tracey as she stood with her plastic tray resting on the polished metal tubes of the cafeteria line.

Linda Luongo reached for a limp tunafish sandwich, which she plopped down next to her five-cent bag of potato chips, and slid her tray forward. "I always thought he was the smartest kid I ever knew," she said. "Even smarter than a lot of adults."

"I know. So did I, even if I didn't always admit it. I remember the first spelling bee we had in that class when he wiped everyone out. The words! I mean . . . *pernicious*, and *resuscitate*, and *verisimilitude*, for goodness sakes! And then today."

Plunging a straw in her milk carton and moving toward their table, Linda turned to Marilyn and said, "You won't believe this, but I think he knew how to spell it all along. But he just didn't *remember* at that moment. Maybe that's it."

"And maybe he's just not so smart after all," said Marilyn. "There he goes now, out to the playground. I guess he's skipping lunch to study for this afternoon. I'll bet the only reason he always seemed so smart is 'cause he studied all the time. Then the election came up and he didn't have so much time to study. I bet a lot of us are just as smart as him."

"Oh, you think so?" asked Lester, who had moved into the seat next to her as she filled her mouth with bread and bologna. "When was the last time you won a spelling bee? 'Sides, it wasn't such a easy word, you know. Two others got it wrong after him."

"Oh, yeah?" asked Howie, who had been listening halfheartedly. "What was the word?"

"Complacency," said Marilyn. "Just an ordinary word."

Dolly Sutter was disappointed at first. She was looking forward to Martin's visit as a pleasant break in her weekly routine. And, even though she only expected a brief chat with him, he seemed distant when he delivered the order that she had telephoned to his father's store that morning. No time for tea. No time for talk.

"Is everything all right?" she had asked. "How's the campaign going?"

"Everything's fine," he had murmured, and then he had slipped through the doorway and dashed off.

Something tells me that everything isn't so rosy, she thought and headed for the telephone, where she dialed the Martinson household.

By the time Lester arrived the next morning, Martin had already left for school.

"I don't know what's come over him, Lester," said Mrs. Martinson. "Yesterday, he stopped off at the store again and then delivered a few packages for his father. He took one up to the Sutters, but he didn't stay there very long, no siree. And he didn't come right home afterward, either. When I asked him where he'd been, he just said that he'd just 'hung around.' But he didn't say where or with whom. Do you know what he's up to?"

"No, ma'am," said Lester, blinking at her through his glasses. "I dunno, but something's funny. Maybe if I run I can catch up with him and find out." And off he went.

Lester had just reached the old fence at the far edge of the back field when he noticed a patch of light blue poplin that didn't fit in with the landscape. On a hunch, he hiked over and was rewarded. There, crouched behind a big rock and an overgrowth of brambles, sat Martin, staring into the distance. If his jacket hadn't been open and a corner flipping in the wind, no one would have ever seen him.

Lester approached cautiously.

"Hey, Martin, whatcha doing? Why didn't you wait for me this morning? I wasn't late."

"Oh, Les, I . . . ," Martin stammered as he recognized the intruder. "I didn't mean anything. I just felt like getting out of the house a little early. Everyone asking questions and talking about the election and everything. I just wanted time to think."

"Gee, I'm sorry if I interrupted you."

"Hey, no, that's okay. We've gotta get going anyhow. Don't want to be late for good old school," Martin replied sarcastically.

They walked silently for a few minutes, kicking the random stone or branch that happened to be in their path. Finally, Lester just stopped and turned to Martin.

"Hey, what's the matter with you, anyhow?"

"What do you mean?"

"You know. What's goin' on? All this moody and silent stuff. And doing lousy in school. The spelling bee. And I heard what happened in your math class. History, too. Everywhere. All of a sudden you don't know anything. It's like you've got magnesia."

"*Am*nesia."

"See, I knew your brain was working," Lester shouted. "I did that on purpose. You haven't gone dumb by accident or anything; you're doing it on purpose."

"Shut up, Lester."

"Marty-Smarty, hah! Marty-Wiseguy."

"Take a break, Lester, I . . . I . . . I, oh, golly, I don't know what I'm doing anymore. You're right. I am doing it deliberately. I just don't know what else to do. If everyone is convinced that I'm so smart I can't be a regular guy like everyone else, I figured maybe I ought to show them I could be, well, not-so-smart. If I could do just a little less than usual, maybe they would kind of get it into their heads that I was okay, after all."

"Aw, Martin." Lester spoke gently. "That was a pretty good idea. But I guess it didn't work because everyone expects so much of you in school that when you don't do so good, it looks awful instead. You should have heard Marilyn Tracey yesterday. All of a sudden she didn't think you were so smart. But she didn't like you any more than she did before. 'Fact, I don't think anyone would vote for you 'cause you're dumb any more than they would 'cause you're smart."

131

"That's just it, Les. And I couldn't keep it up, anyhow. You don't know how much it takes to be wrong when you know the right answers."

"C'mon, Martin, we'd better speed it up a little. Listen, there's got to be some other way. The election is next week. We still have a little time. Want to meet right after school and talk about it?"

"I can't."

"Why not?"

"I promised my mother I'd help her do errands. She just told me about it this morning. But later on, maybe after supper, I'll come over to your house. I'll call you. We've gotta come up with an idea."

Chapter 16

The last three steps of the back porch seemed to groan in protest under the slight weight of the boy and the wicker basket filled with its moist burden. Too many years of snow and rain, followed by exposure to the afternoon sun, had made those old steps crotchety, he thought.

"Here it is, the last load," Martin said as he put the basket down next to his mother. She was standing in front of the open framework of the vast wooden stretchers that she used for drying and stretching the fragile curtains that went up and down in the living room like the seasons.

"I don't know why I kept putting this off," she mused, half talking to Martin, half to herself. "But thank goodness we have a nice sunny day and these will be dry soon enough. Doesn't take the heat long to get into these flimsy things."

"Thought we were going to do errands," grumbled Martin.

"That's because you weren't listening. I said I needed some help this afternoon and you assumed I meant errands. Lately, I don't think you're all there when I'm talking to you, Martin. And I think it's about time you let us know what on earth is troubling you. Your father and I are very concerned about your behavior. Now, would you like to come upstairs and have another glass of milk or something?"

"No, thanks," he replied, looking down at the ground.

"Well, then, I have another idea," she said, brightly. "You go on and finish your homework. Go ahead, get it done now. I have plans and you won't have time later on. Come on, upstairs."

"But . . ."

"No 'buts' about it. Sometimes you ask too many questions. Just . . ."

"I know, 'Just listen to your mother.'" He smiled. "Hey, is this it? Are we going to make fudge tonight?"

"Just as I thought, you're not so smart after all. Now stop your guessing and start your studying. I hear you need a little work in spelling," she said, giving him a tap on the bottom as they climbed the creaky stairs together.

"I hate spareribs."

"Never say you *hate* any food, Helena. Remember

the starving Armenians," scolded Mrs. Martinson as she surveyed the menu.

The red and gold walls and the black lacquered booth with plastic seats enclosed the three of them as they scanned the exotic listing and decided to order. Despite Helena's objections, Mrs. Martinson ordered the spareribs, which she and Martin enjoyed, plus the egg roll, which they could do without but which Helena liked. They also asked for Chicago chow mein, which came with crisp noodles, mushroom chow yuk, because they all loved the thin slices of beef and mushrooms in the aromatic brown sauce, and fried rice, the perfect accompaniment to everything.

"Remember the first time we came here and Dad tried to use chopsticks?" Martin commented. "Boy, was that funny."

"Yes, we all laughed because he loves Chinese food so much and he just couldn't get anything to his mouth without dropping it first," Mrs. Martinson replied.

"Too bad he couldn't be here tonight," said Helena.

"Oh, I'm sure he'll have a decent meal at his lodge. And anyhow, I thought we deserved a restaurant meal, just the three of us. How long has it been since I've had my two little babies out for a night on the town?"

"Aw, Mom, don't start that mushy stuff," said Martin.

"Why not? You are my babies and always will be,

even when you're . . . oh, fifty years old, you know. But I don't treat you like babies, now, do I? Tell the truth."

"Nope," said Helena, picking daintily at the crisp edge of an egg roll. "You really don't bother us a lot like some mothers do. You ought to hear Nancy's mother talk to her."

"And Lester's mother, too."

"Well, the point is that it's not important how your friends' parents act toward their children. Your father and I feel that you're both old enough and intelligent enough to know what to do and how to behave in just about any situation. And, if there's anything you don't understand, or don't know what to do, we hope you'll come to us without us pushing you or forcing you. Could you reach that soy sauce, dear?" she asked, nodding toward Helena.

In the quiet that followed, the distant plinkety-plink music coming through the speakers that were tucked into the corners of the ceiling and walls grew more remote. The dim light made shadowy figures of the quiet waiters padding about from table to kitchen and back, and conversations at the other tables seemed to become softer, too. The sound of the silence at their table grew.

Martin put down his fork and wiped a few stray grains of rice from below his bottom lip. He folded his napkin carefully and looked across the table at his mother.

"It's me," he said. "I know you want to know what's bothering me and I know I should talk to you about it, but I don't know what to say."

"Martin, dear, you don't have to say anything. We all know that you're going through a lot of stress with this election thing and I thought it would be fun for you and Helena and me to have this night off. That's all. Please don't feel you have to say anything. Especially to people who love you as we do."

Her words touched a soft spot. All the emotion, the hopes, and frustrations of the last few weeks hit him at the same time and he felt as though he would start to cry right there at the table. But that would be too embarrassing. " 'Scuse me," he said and dashed off in the direction of the men's room.

"Oh, gosh, Mom, do you think he's all right? I mean, if he isn't, who's going to go in after him to find out?" asked Helena.

"Don't you worry," Mrs. Martinson said. "I think this may be just what he needed. A good purging. He thinks he's too old to have these feelings, but once in a while they just happen. There's nothing wrong with a healthy cry every now and then. As long as you don't make a habit and don't indulge yourself in self-pity all the time. Besides, maybe he just had to go to the bathroom."

"Oh, come on, Mom. Honest, what do you think will happen? Will he be all right?"

"I think he'll be just fine. I think your brother is

going to surprise you, and in fact, all of us. It's the unexpected that makes you children so much fun," she said dryly.

"Like when I got chicken pox the time we went to New York," Helena said.

"That's not exactly what I mean," her mother answered. "Here he comes now, so don't say anything silly. Hello, dear, everything all right?" she asked as she saw his shiny, freshly washed face.

"I'm fine," he said. "Listen, it'll be too late to go over to Lester's house when I get back, but do you think I could just call him?"

"Don't they have an 'after ten' rule over there?" asked Helena.

"Well, if they do, we'll just make sure we're back well before that. Now, who wants the last of this chow mein and the noodles?"

She reached forward and began to spoon some into each of their plates.

Chapter 17

It was so nice out, they decided to hold the meeting on Lester's back porch. Soda cases and storage boxes were used as seats for a few; Howie and Stevie sat cross-legged on the plank floor, with their backs leaning up against the clapboard wall.

"OK, everyone," Martin started, "I know you want to get this over with since it's Saturday. But I figure I ought to tell you what's going on and how I figure things are going to work out from now on."

" 'Bout time," piped up Stevie. "Boy, you sure've been acting kind of loony lately, if you know what I mean."

"Yeah," said Bobby. "Like my father says, you keep blowing hot and cold."

"Wait a minute, wait a minute," Lester broke in. "Let's give the candidate a chance."

"The candidate!" said Howie. "Listen to Mr. Bigshot Campaign Manager."

"Okay, guys, just listen for a minute. All right?" said Martin.

They grunted assent.

He went on, "I know I've sort of left you out of what's been going on last week, but I didn't do it to be mean or anything. I just had to try something different to . . . well, to get some attention. And it didn't turn out exactly the way I planned."

"You mean acting dumb and everything?" said Howie.

"You didn't fool anyone," said Bernie. "I figured you were faking, but I didn't want to say anything."

"Maybe you should have," answered Martin. "Maybe friends should tell you when you're doing something stupid. 'Cause that really was. Instead of people liking me better because I wasn't so smart, everyone kept looking at me like I was a real dope."

He looked around at the group and saw them as they were at that moment. Tall, short, neat and messy, pale, dark, pimply — all different, but all the same in one respect. They were his friends and he knew he could count on them. So he continued.

"Well, that's all over with, and to tell you the truth, I really thought of dropping out of the election. I started to think it was a dumb idea to begin with. But then, I thought, hey, that would be quitting without ever knowing what could happen.

"And then I began to realize that that's what's most important. Just going on with it and finishing the

140

job. And that if I do that, I'll get one thing I wanted from the start, too."

"What's that?" asked Stevie.

"For people to know who I am and . . . well, to sort of know that I'm okay."

"You mean to *respect* you, don'tcha," said Lester, more as a statement than a question.

"Yes," Martin answered quietly. "Just the same way you all know me and even when you're mad at me for something, we're still friends because we know each other. I guess that's respect. Because that's the way I feel about you guys, only I never thought I would ever say so."

No one said a word. As they sat listening to their friend they could also hear the sounds outside. Feet slushing through the leaves of the old horse chestnut tree. Traffic horns. Cars turning corners and streetcars screeching along well-worn tracks. They were aware of all of this, but their thoughts were focused on the boy sitting on the packing case, scuffling the frayed toe of his left sneaker with his good right one.

Finally, the high-pitched sound of Lester's voice cut through.

"Okay, okay, that's fine, but what are we going to do to win this election?"

They all made noises of enthusiastic agreement at once.

"All right," said Martin more confidently. "The candidate, as Lester says, has an idea and I'm going to put it to you, and let's hear what you have to say about it. What do you think of this?

"First of all, we've been taking it too easy and making mistakes. For one thing, we've been counting ourselves out of it too fast. And we haven't been doing enough just plain work. We have to really get going. We have to make signs and put them up everywhere. Wherever we can."

"Like the playground fence," said Bobby.

"Like there and how about all the bulletin boards, on every floor?" asked Bernie.

"Can we? I mean, is it OK to use the school bulletin boards?" asked Stevie.

"Why not? They're supposed to be for 'items of common interest.' It says so right underneath them," answered Lester.

Martin continued to outline his plans. They involved a lot of visible campaigning — buttons, posters, stopping friends and acquaintances and asking and reminding them about Martin.

"The last thing," he finished, "the very last is the rally. The rally in the assembly hall is the last chance anybody has to tell the class anything. We each get five minutes in front of everyone in the auditorium."

"Geez," said Howie, "that's a long time. I never stood up in front of anyone and talked that long."

"Well, it's really not long enough for what I want to say, but that's all they give you. I figure once and for all that's the best shot I'll ever have to really get across to people. So this is going to be our last official

142

meeting. I mean, we'll all make posters and things, but I'm going to have to do some real hard work on that speech. I want you to know about it so that you won't think I'm hiding out or anything. OK?"

"Hey, Martin, the only thing we're going to be thinking is that we've got one swell friend who's going to make one swell class president," said Howie. "Right, guys?"

"Right." They jumped up, pushing and jostling, and soon began to wrestle Martin to the floor of the porch.

"Hey, you guys, wait a minute. It's five to one, no fairs."

"Martin, everything's fair in politics," shouted Lester as he grabbed on to a flailing leg.

Chapter 18

The next few days passed in a flurry of activity. Martin and his friends made signs and posters and erected them early in the morning on their way to school and before classes started. The next day there were bigger and bolder signs put up by Normie Sands and his gang.

The Martinson forces decided to confront the main issue in his campaign material and adopted the slogan:

LOOK SMART, ACT SMART, BE SMART —
VOTE FOR MARTY MARTINSON!

The Sands team immediately followed with a blunt statement of where they stood:

ICE CREAM SODAS AND MARCHING BANDS,
CAST YOUR VOTE FOR
N*O*R*M*I*E S*A*N*D*S

144

During lunchtime, there were no more milk-case gatherings, but there was plenty of politicking. Sides were rigidly taken and only the arrival of gray, rainy weather kept the schoolyard from becoming an out-and-out political battlefield. The contest between Martin and Normie Sands had touched off a passion for political competition that had never been experienced at Taft. All candidates were suddenly active and vigorous in their efforts to convince classmates that they were the best choice for the offices of president, vice-president, secretary, or treasurer.

"I'll be glad when the rally comes and goes and this election with it," groaned Mr. Lindstrom one afternoon. "It's becoming the biggest thing here since . . . since . . . since we cut the ribbon on the new gymnasium. Now everyone wants to hear what the candidates have to say in their closing campaign speeches. Can you imagine this? I received a call from the Glendale *Beacon* to ask if they could send a reporter to the rally."

"Oh, Mr. Lindstrom," squealed one of the secretaries, "can we go, too?"

The sun decided to make an appearance the morning of the rally. It beamed down on the well-scrubbed, well-polished boy and his friend, who walked slowly but deliberately along the paved streets, avoiding the soggy piles of decaying leaves.

"Martin," said Lester, "I know you must be kind of

nervous so I don't want to say anything to remind you of it, but I gotta tell you that I think you're going to do just great."

"You know something, Lester," Martin replied calmly, "I feel just great. I feel as though I've won already and it has nothing to do with how many votes I get."

The two just grinned at each other and continued on toward the school.

Mr. Lindstrom's voice droned on. "And now that you've heard from the candidates from the ninth and eighth grades, it's time for the seventh."

Most of the audience cheered these words. Everyone was aware of the intense rivalry that had awakened the interest of the entire school.

"By a toss of the coin," he announced, "it has been decided that the first speaker we will hear will be the candidate for president, Norman Sands."

Loud cheering, whistles, shouts, and applause.

Normie Sands smiled from ear to ear and walked to the speaker's stand in the middle of the stage.

"My fellow classmates and good friends," he began.

For the next five minutes he read a carefully prepared, grammatically correct speech in which he affirmed his position that it was the school's job to give them an education and the class officers' job to see that they had a good time while they were there learning. It wasn't a frivolous speech, but it stuck to the one point and it outlined Normie's program of a limited dues assessment and as broad a spending of those funds, supplemented by "private contributions," as possible.

He concluded to boisterous applause.

Mr. Lindstrom returned to the center of the stage. "And now, a few words from this young man's opponent. We will now hear from Stanley Martin Martinson, Junior."

More applause and shouts mixed with a few boos and catcalls.

Martin walked calmly to the speaker's stand and put down his speech. He paused, and then he began in a slightly quavering voice, "Mr. Lindstrom, members of the faculty and administration, representatives of the press, schoolmates, and you, my fellow classmates. Although I am running for the office of seventh-grade class president, it is to all of you that I address what I have to say, since you all have an interest in us and we are concerned how your actions affect us.

"The way I look at it, up until now, being a class officer has meant being in charge of planning social activities. 'Leave the teaching to the teachers and the partying to the partygoers.' That's been the unofficial slogan.

"The problem is that this leaves out a lot, the whole middle. That's 'W–H–O–L–E,' for those of you who have heard that I don't spell so well these days."

There was scattered laughter at this remark.

"Anyhow, there's a lot more than just going to

147

classes and going to parties that takes place around Taft. It took me a while to see it, but once I got started, the list just kept growing. There's the seating situation at football games, for starters. How about that?"

Applause and shouts of "What about us?" came from the seventh-grade section.

"There's the broken lockers. And the missing bicycle racks. And the library hours. Or should I say 'minutes'? A half hour a day after school, for everyone, even people on the teams and cheerleaders who have to practice right away."

Loud cheers and applause broke out throughout the auditorium. Everyone was paying attention to him now.

He went on, "You know, when you look around, this is a pretty nice place. But it wouldn't hurt to spruce it up a little. Instead of all that dirt and gravel out front, how about a little grass? I mean, the rich kids aren't the only ones who should have fancy lawns.

"But that, too, is just one side of things. I said I wouldn't ignore the social side because I'm just as interested in a good time as the next person. But I think there should be fewer parties for just the so-called 'in crowd' and more for everyone. Because, when Taft wins a game, it's everyone who should share in that win. And we shouldn't be afraid to plan a party which will have to take place even if we lose.

Because that's all part of being here at Taft, the good, the bad and anything in between.

"What I'm saying is that instead of being a patsy little job for the most popular person in the class, I think the president's job is a big one. It's something that can maybe influence and improve things at Taft."

As his time became shorter, he began to wind up his speech.

"So I am asking for your votes, my fellow seventh-graders. With each ballot you cast in my name, you offer a challenge to the" — a long pause while he looked around the room and zeroed in his eyes on Marilyn Tracey — "the *complacency* which has gripped this school for too long.

"And if I am elected, I will not ignore that challenge, the same one that has been laid before every public servant since the times of earliest civilization: to respond to and to serve those who put them in office. You all know what happened to Julius Caesar. . . ."

The audience broke into laughter.

"Well, don't forget what happened to those who came after him. They all got theirs, too."

Even greater laughter.

"So, in closing, I would like to say just one more thing. I would like to thank all those who have worked closely with me during this campaign, my special friends Lester and Howie and Bernie and Bobby and Stevie . . . and all the rest who helped out.

We have shared and learned something that I hope all of you will know some day. And that is that just participating in the democratic process automatically makes you a winner, no matter how the count comes out. Thank you all very much."

"Well," said Mrs. Burns to Mrs. McManus, sitting in the back row, "what do you think of your bright young man now?"

"Lordy," she replied, "all I wanted was a proper attitude toward his mathematics. It looks as though we may have gotten more than we bargained for with that boy."

Chapter 19

There was great excitement as the entire school filed out of the auditorium and returned to their homerooms for the close of school and for the balloting. Tension ran highest in the seventh grade, since everyone wanted to know: could Martinson beat Sands?

Stevie caught up with Lester and Martin as they turned the corner out of the schoolyard.

"Hey guys," he yelled as he approached, "you want to play some stickball this afternoon? I'm meeting Howie later on."

"Sure," said Lester, "me and Martin against you and Howie, for starters. Let's get Bernie and Bobby and whoever else is around."

"Right," said Martin, "Why not? No more politics. Hooray!"

They had just finished eating their main course and Martin was looking forward to dessert when Mrs.

Martinson made what was for her a surprising confession.

"Oh, dear, I've been so busy I just didn't have a chance to make dessert. But I have an idea. How would you two like to take a walk over to Sorenson's and bring back a quart of vanilla ice cream? While you're gone I'll make some fudge sauce and we can have home-made sundaes."

"What about cleaning up?" asked Martin.

"Oh, your father and I can do that in a jiffy. Now, here's a dollar. You two run along."

"But why do we both have to go?" he continued. "I'm old enough to go by myself."

"Martin, stop asking a million questions. Take a walk with your sister and be grateful that I'm going to do the dishes," Mr. Martinson said.

"Come on, silly," said Helena. "Last one out the door is a pinhead."

They sped off on the short walk to the drugstore, teasing each other playfully and enjoying the after-dinner exercise. On the way back, Helena kept lagging behind and Martin had to remind her that they were carrying ice cream. It would melt if they didn't hurry. But she didn't speed up. He felt that it was only his pressing that got the ice cream home before it was soup.

It was quiet in the hallway as they climbed the stairs. Martin figured that his mother and father had just finished doing the dishes and were reading the newspaper waiting for them to get back. I hope the fudge sauce is all made, he thought as he turned the doorknob.

"Surprise!"

A crowd of voices burst as the door was opened. There were crepe-paper streamers and the table was spread with a cake and candles and bright paper plates and napkins. And the whole place was filled with people. Lester. Howie. Stevie and Bobby and Bernie. And Rick Petersen. And Mrs. Sutter with some man who turned out to be Mr. Sutter. And even Old Frank!

Helena was smiling and blushing at the same time, but she wasn't too timid to give Martin a little push inside the door. Mr. and Mrs. Martinson came over and gave him big hugs and then he was passed from person to person. The boys all gave him hearty handshakes and strong pats on the back. Mrs. Sutter kissed his cheek and he gave her a warm hug.

When he completed the circuit, Mrs. Martinson made him sit at the head of the table where his father usually sat.

"Now, dear," she explained, "we figured that you had learned an important lesson about politics with this election. You know, what you said in your speech about participation being the important thing? So, we figured that if you could understand that, we should show you that you're right. This is a 'participation party,' not a victory, or even a consolation, party. And we wanted everyone who helped you especially to come. So, Dolly and Mr. Sutter . . ."

153

"Herb," he reminded her.

"Right. Herb," she went on. "They were in charge of decorations and they were right across the street waiting for you and Helena to leave. And the minute you were out the door, we called Lester and he called the boys and so on and on. . . ."

"I just got here in the nick of time," piped up Old Frank. "Saw you two comin' round the corner and I hotfooted it up those stairs. Knocked on the door and you could have heard a pin drop inside till they saw it was me."

"Hey, Martin, how's about a speech," shouted Stevie across the room.

"Gosh, uh, gee . . . I . . . well," Martin started out, but the pleasure of having this group of people celebrating with him caused a big lump in his throat. "Well," he went on, "well . . . thank you for coming . . . and . . . hey, the ice cream is going to melt!"

"And," said Mrs. Martinson, "we don't want melted ice cream on our chocolate cake, now, do we?"

Chapter 20

"Too bad, Martinson, just three votes," he heard as he stood in front of the bulletin board. It *would* be Marilyn Tracey giving him the news.

"Uh huh," he replied, staring at the notice which appeared to be going in and out of focus. It almost seemed to be impossible that there should be a piece of paper on it and that two-thirds of the way down there would be:

Seventh Grade

For president:	Sands	62
	Martinson	59

Lester gave him a nudge. "It's the closest contest in the whole school. Everybody else won by a landslide, but we really gave 'em a run for it."

We? thought Martin, We? I'm the one who lost. I'm the one who thought he was so smart he could win. I'm the one who everyone will think of as a failure. I'm the one who'll drag all my friends down to disgrace with me.

He didn't know what to do, where to turn. It was too early to go to his homeroom, but he couldn't stand in front of that bulletin board any longer. He wanted to run somewhere, to hide his disappointment from everyone. But it was too late. A crowd had gathered behind and around him. They stared at the notice and began to make comments. He was ready to bolt when he looked up and saw Mr. Lindstrom coming toward the board and staring at him.

"Too bad, Martinson, just three votes," said Mr. Lindstrom, the perfect echo of Marilyn Tracey. "Well," he went on, "that's the sad part of politics. Qualified individuals don't always gain the confidence of the electorate the first time around. I trust that you are not going to let your defeat prevent you from future contests in the political arena, hmmm?"

"Uh, no sir, well, that is, I mean, I don't know; I haven't really thought about it," Martin mumbled as the students around him stood in silent awe of the principal.

"Of course, it's too soon and the shock is undoubtedly still very much present. But I'm sure you will come around and we can expect student government to benefit from your presence in the future."

"Yes, sir. I'll try to think that way, sir."

"Good. And while you're trying, I think you may be pleased at another announcement I'm going to make today. That is that we are going to appoint one student from each class to represent his classmates at the general council of the Parent–Teachers Association. They will form the nucleus of what will become a PTSA eventually, to work for the betterment of some conditions in the school. Now, I don't want you to think that this is some kind of consolation prize, but the faculty has recommended your appointment to represent the seventh grade.

"We've been working on this for some time, and it is merely coincidental that the announcement will follow the election results. Of course, everyone will assume that it *is* a consolation gesture, but you're capable of dealing with that, aren't you?"

"Yes, sir! You bet, sir," said Martin, beaming.

"Fine. the announcement will be out today and our first meeting will be the second Wednesday in November. Hmmm, that's just around the corner. Better get on with your schoolwork so that you can spare the time. And you, the rest of you," he said as he turned about, "why are you all standing around? Into your homerooms. Let's get on with things. This is a school, you know."

As they began to go their separate ways, Lester looked up at Martin and said, "This is even better than president, Martin. I knew you'd come out on top, somehow."

"Wait a minute," said Martin. "It isn't *better*, it's just different. Gee, I hope everyone won't think I'm getting too big for my britches, meeting with the PTA and everything."

157

"I wouldn't worry about it, Martin. 'Sides, I hear all they do at those PTA meetings is pick on the principal and the school committee. You ought to be good at that."

Martin threw an arm around his friend and said, "Hey, Les, as soon as I take over the PTA, maybe I'll run for governor. How would you like to be my campaign manager; you did such a great job on this election? Huh? Huh?"